CARIBBEAN SUNSET WITH A YELLOW PARROT

Lady Amanda Golightly and her old friend Hugo Cholmondley-Crichton-Crump are off to the Caribbean. One of Lady A's old school-friends is having a school reunion and is also trying to sell the villas she has built on part of a privately-owned island. Some of the old girls already live there, others are crossing for the reunion by sea on the Seven Seas Floating Party Town. Life is eventful. Soon after disembarkation, the tropical island is rife with murder, smuggling, blackmail and much, much, more. Lady Amanda and Hugo are off on the detecting trail once more – and their adventures include Hugo's unfortunate experience with the local hot sauce.

CARIBBEAN SUNSET WITH A YELLOW PARROT

by

Andrea Frazer

Magna Large Print Books
Long Preston, North Yorkshire,
BD23 4ND, England.

British Library Cataloguing in Publication Data.

A catalogue record of this book is
available from the British Library

ISBN   978-0-7505-4425-2

First published in Great Britain by Accent Press 2014

Published in Large Print 2017 by arrangement with
Accent Press

Magna Large Print is an imprint of Library Magna Books Ltd.

Printed and bound in Great Britain by
T.J. (International) Ltd., Cornwall, PL28 8RW

DRAMATIS PERSONAE

School Reunion-goers

Lady Amanda Golightly – Sniffy
Hermione Bazalgette – Horseface
Deirdre Brokenshire – Droopy-Drawers
Wendy Godiva – Wuffles
Douglas Huddlestone-Black – Adonis
Letitia Littlechild – Longshanks
Ffion Simpson – Fflageolet

Other Passengers on the *Seven Seas Floating Party Town*

Hugo Cholmondley-Crichton-Crump – friend of
  Sniffy Golightly
Beauchamp – butler-cum-general factotum to
  Sniffy
Enid Beauchamp – bride of the butler and friend
  of Sniffy

Residents of the Parrot Bay Sundowners' Retirement community

Belinda   Bartholomew – Butterfingers, of
  Tropical Hideaway – 11
Caroline Cassidy – Hopalong, of Coconut
  Corner – 2
Dorothy Leclerc – Hefferlump, of The Palms – 9

Philippa Montrose – Eeyore, of West Indies
   Retreat – 14
Cecelia Nosegay – Snotty, of Lagoon View – 12A
Wendy Winterbottom – Windy, of Cocktails – 16
Julian Morris – aka Morris Minor & Beep-Beep,
   of Cocktails – 16

Other Island Residents

Albert 'Albie' Ross – runs the Parakeet Club
Winstone Churchill – local bus driver
Short John Silver – runs Old Uncle Obediah's
   Rum Keg Landing beach bar

Prologue

The cough from the back of the church had reverberated with the impact of heavy artillery shot, halting the wedding and drawing all eyes to its source at the important point where the vicar had called for anyone present to speak now, or forever hold his peace.

The bride, Enid Tweedie, widow of this parish and friend and gofer for Lady Amanda Golightly, and the groom, Beauchamp, butler to the same, stood whey-faced and open-mouthed at the front of the church, while every mind in the building whirred with activity. Was there something in Beauchamp's past which no one knew about? Was he a bigamist? Come to that, was Enid a bigamist, perhaps never having been widowed?

The man at the back coughed again, his hand in front of his mouth to prove he had been a well-brought-up boy, and cleared his throat, preparatory to speaking. Here was the truth. What were they about to learn, to sweeten and enliven Belchester's already busy gossip mill?

'I do apologise,' he said, only heightening the tension. What did he want to apologise for? Was he a player in whatever he was about to reveal? He cleared his throat again and continued, 'Mark Morton, church warden. I seem to have inhaled a small insect. Please carry on. I'm very sorry to have interrupted. Forgive me, and do carry on.'

A collective sigh of disappointment that as held breaths were exhaled made enough of a breeze to stir Morton's hat, and a buzz of let-down conversation began to move through the body of the church.

The vicar also coughed, to drag everyone's attention back to the matter at hand, then carried on with the service, his voice a little wobbly, as if this interruption had severely upset him, while a snort of indignation could be heard from the matron of honour, Lady Amanda herself, wearing what she referred to as 'a pastel-coloured meringue'.

The rest of the service went off without a hitch, as did the photographs outside the church, the only outré moment being when the man with the camera asked the ladies present to show a bit of leg for a risqué shot. Lady Amanda slightly uncovered what looked like a sturdy leg of pork, while Enid pulled her wedding dress high enough to show off her garter, revealing several nicotine patches nestling underneath it: a novelty, to say the least. A mass clicking indicated that most of the guests also wished to capture this unusual sight for posterity.

It was not too long, though, before the wedding party returned to Belchester Towers, the ancestral home of Lady Amanda's family, for the wedding breakfast.

The caterers had been back, as had the wedding decorators, and the place was transformed into a fairytale celebration venue, starting with white ribbons, bows, and balloons at the front steps. Inside, every surface was covered in flowers, from dirty great vasefuls to tiny little nosegays; there was white ribbon everywhere, and balloons bobbed like captive clouds, tied to just about every piece of furniture.

The theme of each table centre was a heart, and these sprouted from place cards to menu holders, too. All in all, Cinderella didn't just go to the ball, it was thrown in her honour, and Enid went pink with delight when she set eyes on it, making little squeaking noises of approval and disbelief.

The toastmaster, who was part of the catering package, started off the ceremony by explaining the order of events, which ended with carriages at three a.m., and introduced Beauchamp, that he may welcome his guests and introduce his bride to all here gathered. There were no parents-in-law to introduce, although he did give hearty thanks to his employer, who had made a gift of this reception and the honeymoon to the happy couple. Enid blushed again at the implications of the word 'honeymoon', but Beauchamp carried on regardless.

'I and my, um, wife, er, have told everyone that we were going to the West Country for this part of the getting married experience.' Here, Enid nodded contentedly, before he continued, 'Instead of which, due to my employer, Lady Amanda Golightly's incredible generosity we are going, not to that delightful part of the country, but, to the West Indies.'

Enid spilt champagne all down the front of her frock in shock, and accidentally inhaled the mouthful she was about to swallow. While Hugo Cholmondley-Crichton-Crump thumped her

11

back, murmuring, 'There, there, old girl. Cough it up, and you'll feel much better,' there was a communal sharp intake of breath from the guests, which was repeated, fortissimo, when Beauchamp carried on with his speech.

'We are going to a tiny island which is privately owned, called Caribbaya. Lady Amanda and Mr Hugo will accompany us on our sea journey across the Atlantic, whereafter they will stay with one of her ladyship's old schoolfriends, and my bride and I shall retire to separate guest accommodation.'

The hubbub rose in volume. The old wrinklies were going on honeymoon with them? How absolutely disastrous. How could the newlyweds stomach the thought of being at their beck and call all the way over on that long sea crossing, then no doubt summoned from their guest accommodation at all hours, to pass the salt or something just as ridiculous?

Lady Amanda sat smirking like the Cheshire cat, Hugo had resumed his seat and looked thoroughly embarrassed, while Enid, the new Mrs Beauchamp, now had hiccoughs, and her eyes stared widely as if her whole world had just shattered around her.

'Beechy?' she croaked, holding out a hand to her new husband.

'Later,' he reassured her, patting the hand, and handing over to the best man.

Chapter One

Their luggage was all packed, and they break-fasted as normal on sailing day, as the boat didn't leave until four in the afternoon. The next morning, an army of cleaners would descend on Belchester Towers to get it spick and span, fit for their return in three weeks' time. Today, all four of them breakfasted together, Enid still getting used to the idea that she would be spending her honeymoon with the 'Saga louts' for whom she and her new husband worked.

Although she hoped against hope that they could have some kind of privacy, she didn't trust those two not to ferret out some murder or other malfeasance, and drag her and Beauchamp into the jaws of danger as they had done on four previous occasions.

'What is the name of this cruise liner you have booked for us?' asked Beauchamp, swallowing a mouthful of bacon and breaking the awkward silence that was currently prevailing. Hugo was also uncharacteristically quiet, being in a bit of a sulk, not only because he had not been consulted about whether he wanted to go or not, but also because he thought it was intrusive and pre-sumptuous of Manda to include the two of them on what was, after all, someone else's *honeymoon*, for God's sake!

'It's the one that Windy Winterbottom said

everyone else was coming over on, for this school reunion,' replied Lady Amanda, sipping her coffee, oblivious to how everyone else was feeling. All was right in her world, and her skin was so thick that artillery shells could not have pierced it.

'Windy?' squeaked Enid, who had returned to her normal self now, through deep breathing and the use of nicotine patches, and re-joined the land of the non-smokers. She was retrospectively proud of the fact that she had had five patches under her wedding garter, to prevent nerves which might tempt her back to the wicked weed.

'Oh, her real name is Wendy. We all had nicknames at school.'

'What was yours?' ventured a rather bold Beauchamp.

'Well, I might as well tell you, as you'll find out anyway. I was known as Sniffy Golightly, because I suffered from a constantly runny nose, which turned out, on inspection by a doctor when I was nine years old, to be the result of a plastic bead, which I must have pushed up there when I was a mere toddler. Anyway, the name stuck for the rest of my schooldays.'

'How dreadful,' sympathised Enid.

'I know,' replied Lady A. 'Fancy my mother letting me get my hands on anything made of plastic!'

This was hardly the answer Enid expected, but she carried on gamely with her enquiries. 'And who are the others going to the reunion?'

'Let me see, ooh yes, Hermione Bazalgette, Deirdre Brokenshire, Wendy Godiva, yummy Douglas Huddlestone-Black, who was the headmistress's son, Letitia Littlechild, and Ffion Simpson will all be on the same vessel.

'When we get there, we will meet Belinda Bartholomew, Cecelia Nosegay – silly name – Dorothy Leclerc and Caroline Cassidy. Windy and her partner – never met him – got hold of the land, then those four put in money for villas for themselves, and the rest of the close was built, to represent the start of the Parrot Bay Sundowners Community for the Retired. I believe that only Parrot Bay is built at the moment, but there are great plans to expand – clubhouse, that sort of thing, I believe.'

'And that vessel is called?' Beauchamp ploughed on doggedly – he wasn't giving up that easily.

'And do they all have nicknames, too?' asked Enid, at the same time. The atmosphere was becoming a little less glacial, and there was danger of a little excitement leaking in around its melting edges, for none of them had been to the Caribbean before and, even with Lady A and Hugo in tow, it was a hugely enticing thought that, within a few days, they could be sprawled on a tropical beach with a tall cool glass of rum punch in their hands.

'Of course they do, dear Enid, but you shall find those out when you meet them.'

'The name of the vessel, your ladyship?' Beauchamp soldiered on, wondering what she was hiding.

'I've booked a suite for Hugo and I. We will have to share, but there are two queen-sized beds...'

'Manda!' spluttered Hugo, covering his front with toast crumbs, suddenly appalled, his equi-

15

librium totally capsized.

'And I have booked a double cabin for you two. Inside, because I doubt you'll spend much time looking out of a window, will you?' she said with a sly wink in Enid and Beauchamp's direction. As her mother had always said, you don't look at the mantelpiece when you're poking the fire, and the same went for portholes and new brides, in her opinion.

This embarrassingly intimate question effectively silenced everyone but Beauchamp. 'The name? What is the name of the blasted ship?'

'For your information,' announced Lady Amanda, 'Mr Nosy-Parker Looking-A-Gift-Horse-In-The-Mouth Beauchamp, the name of the blasted ship is the *Seven Seas Floating Party Town*.' She then lived up to her school nickname by giving the most enormous sniff, as if daring any of those present to question her choice of vessel.

Beauchamp had loaded the extraordinary amount of luggage they seemed to be taking with them into the Rolls, even pushing squashy travelling bags into the back seat with Lady Amanda and Hugo, the former complaining that she felt like part of a left luggage consignment, and would the man please leave her enough room to breathe. Beauchamp gave the last squishy bag a final squeeze, extracting an 'Oh, I say!' from Hugo, before getting into the driver's seat and aiming the vehicle towards the port.

All four of the car's passengers had their heads filled with visions of what the cruise terminal would be like, none of them very realistic, and based mostly on old newsreels and black and

16

white films. To say that each and every one of them romanticised it would be a huge understatement.

The most pessimistic was the new Mrs Beauchamp's, whose mind continued to chew over grainy monochrome images of all the poor people boarding the *Titanic*, off to start a new life in the New World via third class, with no idea of their place in history, and the disaster that was shortly to occur to deprive them of the rest of their lives, never mind their new ones. She had distrusted transatlantic sea crossings ever since she had first heard of this disaster as a child.

When they had sent off the car for long-term parking and checked in their luggage, Lady Amanda looked around her and asked if some of the people milling round might be the showgirls from the entertainment staff. Hugo chipped in with the possibility that there may be a few school trips booked to sail.

Beauchamp gave a loud 'harumph', threw a contemptuous gaze towards his employer, and asked her to repeat the name of the ship.

'I told you at breakfast,' replied Lady Amanda, her gaze as flinty as his was steely. *'The Seven Seas Floating Party Town.'*

'And you wonder who all these young people are?' he asked, making sure that his tone was rhetorical enough even for her selective hearing.

'You mean...' she spluttered. 'You mean that all these children are the actual passengers? But there's not a dowager duchess in sight, and where are all the honourables? Where are the ladies and the sirs? I don't understand.'

'Say the name again, but more slowly this time,

and maybe understanding will dawn on you,' advised the butler.

Lady Amanda's lips moved imperceptibly and, on repeating the word 'Party', she examined the cruise vessel a little more closely. 'It's flying the Stars and Stripes? Why's that? And where's the Union Jack?' she declared loudly.

'Your ladyship has booked an American party boat, the target customer of which is young, heavy on the alcohol, and deep into partying of the more wild variety.'

'You mean there will be no games of charades or bridge? No floating around elegantly on the dancefloor?'

'There will be body-popping and gyrating to heavy drum and bass, and rap – and a bit of nostalgic seventies disco-bopping, *if* your ladyship is lucky. The dancefloor will be a sea of perspiring young bodies, all well over their alcohol limit, in various stages of undress or unconsciousness. They may even be throwing up to the music.'

'You will have your little joke, Beauchamp,' interjected Hugo nervously, when suddenly a voice hailed through the crowds, 'Manda? Sniffy Golightly, is that you?'

A tall, stooped woman with an extraordinarily long face and enormous protruding teeth efficiently elbowed her way through the melee and halted by Hugo's side. 'This the other half, eh, Sniffy? Is he up to snuff? Sniffy; snuff. Ha ha!'

Lady Amanda's brows furrowed at this ridiculous and impertinent question, and addressed the new arrival. 'What ho. Horseface! May I introduce you to Hugo Cholmondley-Crichton-Crump, one

18

of my oldest friends, and to Beauchamp and his new bride Enid; almost like part of the family. Gang, this is Horseface Bazalgette who appeared on the jolly old register as Hermione.'

A 'coo-ee' from several rows behind sounded, and four more elderly ladies pushed their way through to join them. Greetings ensued. 'Hi Sniffy', 'llo Horseface.'

'Jolly hockey sticks, Fflageolet.'

'Wotcher, Wuffles. Have you spotted Adonis yet?'

'Where's Longshanks? Just coming with Droopy-Drawers? Jolly Dee.'

The crowd of mad old women now numbered five, shortly to be joined by a white-haired old boy whom every member of the school reunion greeted with swooning smiles and looks of adoration.

When a woman in ship's uniform came up beside Hugo and offered him a glass of Mimosa, he absentmindedly took two – one with each hand, and immediately drained both glasses, placing them back on the tray to take another two. 'Thanks a million, my dear. I really needed a drink.' With all these bizarre nicknames to cope with, he'd need something a bit stronger than Mimosas to see him through this voyage and holiday.

Everyone was eventually gathered aboard in a vast room where even more Mimosas were the order of the day, and the gaggle of grey and blue-rinsed heads got together once more to say how much they were looking forward to meeting Butterfingers, Snotty, Hefferlump, and Hopalong again.

Hugo, Beauchamp, and Enid surreptitiously shuffled to an adjacent table and sat there in sulky mystification. It felt like they had been marooned on another planet, rather than just boarded a ship. How would they ever get the hang of who was who? And exactly how did they address Lady A now? Would they really be expected to refer to her as Sniffy Golightly? The very idea was unthinkable: anathema.

A public address system began to make announcements in deck order downwards as to which cabins were now ready and accessible to their occupants. Lady Amanda, Hugo, and the braying coven were called almost immediately.

As Hugo trotted up behind his old friend and she opened the door of their suite, the only thing he could think of saying was, 'Oh, cripes, old stick. There may be two beds, but where's the privacy screen? How am I going to get into my jim-jams?'

'You'll change in the bathroom, the same as I will. It's no worse than boarding school was, with all the strange dorm-mates we both must have met in those days,' came an obviously rehearsed retort. 'Wasn't there someone in your dorm who always tried to get into bed with other fellows, claiming he was afraid of the dark or something?'

'Oh yes, I'd forgotten old Wet Rag Wilson. With him, his excuse was spiders, but he was always a bit too free with cuddling up close for safety.'

'And we had Weirdo Smallwood. If it wasn't the dark, it was thunder and lightning with her. Of course, none of us took long to twig what she was

20

up to, then we made her apple-pie beds until she stopped.'

'We put live frogs in Wet Rag's shoes and frogspawn in his bed until he got the message. I suppose, with a bit of effort and forethought, we can rub along quite nicely in here, Manda.'

'Without the actual rubbing along,' replied Lady A shaking her head to shift not only some unpleasant memories from her schooldays, but a ghastly vision of what Hugo's turn of phrase had conjured up. Ugh! She'd never had any time for those sorts of goings on.

The newlyweds had to wait for some time for their deck to be called, and had managed, each, another two Mimosas by then.

At the lift's doors, they discovered that the deck they wanted was not up but down, so they got in, both crossing their fingers that they weren't actually sleeping in staff quarters, and pressed the appropriate button. At the cabin door, which seemed to be very closely flanked on either side by other numbered doors, Beauchamp inserted the key-card and threw open the door onto complete darkness.

He fumbled for the lightswitch, then wished he hadn't. It *may* be a double cabin. It *may not* have a window, being situated deep in the bowels of the ship, but it also *didn't have* a double bed. It had *bunks!*

Dinner was taken by all the Belchester Towers party in-cabin that night – preparing for battle the next morning, in the case of Beauchamp.

21

Chapter Two

At breakfast the next morning the members of the party from Belchester were told that their request for a table for four had been changed to a table for ten. No one could confirm who had made the request, but it looked like all those bound for the island of Caribbaya were to be eating together for the duration of the trans-atlantic crossing, unless otherwise requested.

Hugo took his seat with a face like a slapped arse. He had hoped that they could hide away from all these old biddies, and here he was, marooned with only Beauchamp for male companionship. Douglas Huddlestone-Black was supposed to be sitting with them, but must have chosen to breakfast elsewhere. Stout fellow, thought Hugo, giving it some thought for the other mornings of their cruise. Lady A, of course, was in her element, making contact with that young thing she had been when she was a boarder in the dim and distant past. As a youngster she had lived life more in the raw, but over the years she had developed a veneer of sophistication and decorum which she now felt slightly slipping away.

Enid's face was completely closed, but there were bags under her eyes, and Beauchamp looked like Vesuvius must have appeared just before the big eruption that engulfed Pompeii and Hercu-laneum. It was little short of a miracle that he didn't actually have smoke pouring out of his ears.

'Good morning, Enid. Good morning, Beauchamp,' trilled Lady Amanda, unaware that she was about to be blown to pieces by a hitherto unexploded bomb.

'How dare you!' shouted Beauchamp, turning red and not caring who heard him. 'How bloody dare you pay for this as part of our honeymoon, then book us a cabin with *bunk beds*. How the devil you have the brass-necked cheek to sit there smiling at us when you've done something like that is beyond me, you chiselling old *cheapskate*.'

The object of his fury smiled sweetly at him and replied, 'But I didn't. I booked you a double cabin. There was certainly no mention of bunk beds. There must have been some mix-up with the booking. I shall speak to someone as soon as we have breakfasted. I'm so sorry this has happened, but I expect you'll look back on it, in time, as a rather amusing incident.'

Beauchamp subsided back into his chair, doubting if he would ever feel amused by his mood when he had opened their cabin door last night, but he placed his faith in his employer in sorting out the situation. It did sound like a genuine error.

The formal dining room was small, as most passengers on this ship opted for buffet-style dining, and did not rise much before luncheon. Nevertheless, a limited waiter service was available for those who wished to formalise their eating, and their orders were duly taken, the table soon filling with plates of fried eggs, bacon, mushrooms, sausages, smoked haddock topped with poached eggs, kippers, and eggs Benedict. Side dishes of fried bread, tomatoes and the inevitable pancakes and maple syrup covered any remaining space on the white cloth.

Once the unpleasantness of Beauchamp's furious outburst had settled, it was Lady Amanda who opened the conversation with, 'Are you all going to stay with Windy? She can't have room for us all.'

There were polite little titters around the table, and Wuffles – she of the wild hair and dog-face – explained that they were all going to look at unsold properties in Parrot Bay, and weren't they interested in buying something too? Everyone was being put up in one of the vacant villas, and they would spend some of their time viewing those that were not already sold, and setting up purchases where desired.

'I had no idea Windy was going to do an estate agent's number on us. How many properties are there? Have you all been before?'

'Some of us have,' replied Horseface. 'All the villas that have already sold have sold to old schoolchums just like us. It's a joint venture between Windy and Beep-Beep and the others already living out there helped them to start it. I believe those who have already purchased went out and stayed with Windy to approve the sites.'

'Who in the name of God is Beep-Beep?' asked Lady A, used to the use of nicknames, but never before having tripped over this one.

'His name's Devon Morris,' explained Droopy-Drawers, her snow-white page-boy style bobbed hair nodding, her large breasts almost engulfing the remains of her food on the plate in front of her. 'They met about six or seven years ago, had a whirlwind romance, sold up everything they had between them, and started investing in this island, building all the properties on Parrot Bay. As they sold them, this money would be invested for future development and a modest income for them. At least, I think that's accurate. The idea is definitely to sell the rest of the properties.'

'But why is he called Beep-Beep?' queried Lady Amanda, not in the least interested in the history of the Parrot Bay properties, which she already knew, and more in this unexpected unfamiliar nickname.

Fflageolet fielded this one. 'Because his surname's Morris. Being a younger brother, he was known at school as he was listed on the register – as Morris Minor, hence, this metamorphosed into Beep-Beep, as time went by and his older brother left to go to Oxford.'

Hugo lifted his napkin and buried his face in it in despair. The voices were assaulting his ears from all parts of the table, and the unaccustomed nomenclatures which bothered Manda not a jot were driving him dotty.

'So, if some of the other properties have been sold to other old chums, who's already living there?' Lady Amanda asked out of good manners, as she knew perfectly well who had relocated to this tropical hideaway, but was anxious for no awkward silence to develop, as they had not seen each other for so long.

Now Longshanks took up the explanation. 'Well, apart from Windy and Beep-Beep, there're Hefferlump Leclerc, Butterfingers Bartholomew,

Snotty Nosegay, Hopalong Cassidy and Eeyore Montrose.'

At this point, Hugo actually started wailing, and threw up his hands in despair.

'Don't worry, Mr Cholmondley-Crichton-Crump, Windy knows how confusing it will be for you, so she's producing little lists with everyone's name and nickname, and their house number and name for reference for when we arrive.'

'I shall go one better than that,' declared Beauchamp. 'I shall go to the information desk as soon as possible and ask if we can have some blank badges issued to us, on which each and every one of you can write your nickname, or whatever name you want to be addressed by, and then none of us can make a dreadful faux pas.'

'Splendid idea, Beauchamp, old chap,' chirped Hugo, applauding politely. This sensible gesture should go a little way towards preserving his sanity.

'And I shall suggest that we wear them every mealtime, or whenever we might get together for a trip or for cocktails. We shall all then be well acquainted enough for we three newcomers to this school reunion to concentrate on the fresh nicknames on the island,' the butler commented.

'Where did you get him, Manda? I want one, too.' Wuffles looked longingly at Beauchamp, as if there had never before been anything she had desired so much.

'Hands off! Nobody touches my Beauchamp – except Enid, nowadays.' conceded Lady A with a snide smile. This caused Enid so much fresh embarrassment that she, too, dived into her napkin and hid there, while the rest of the occupants of the table decided what to do next. It looked like she was part of a gang, and she couldn't see any way out of it.

Her new husband and his employer both rose to their feet first. They had, respectively, name badges and bunk beds to sort out ASAP. The general suggestion was that they meet at the pool, and perhaps have a bit of a dip and a short interlude in the sun, and the pair on other missions said they would meet them there.

Still not having formed an accurate judgement of the character of the cruise ship, this did not happen. When Beauchamp arrived on deck with the badges safely stowed in his 'cabin for now', as he thought of it, and Lady Amanda trotted out into the sun knowing that a proper double-bedded cabin was being prepared for Beauchamp and his bride, there was no room to move for barely-clad bodies glistening with suntan oil, all with glasses in hand, swigging on what smelled, even from a distance, of something containing coconut rum.

Every sun lounger was either occupied or covered in someone's towel and belongings, crowds thronged round the bar, and the pool was absolutely heaving with young bodies horsing around. Reggae music blared from loudspeakers cunningly placed so that the cacophony could be heard from every corner of the pool deck.

A svelte waiter with slicked-down hair sidled up to them and asked if he could get them a cocktail. 'At this hour?' questioned Lady Amanda, aghast at this lack of good form.

'You are on a party boat now. No rules, lady. You have exactly what you want, anytime of day.' At this, he had the audacity to wink at her and nudge her gently in the ribs.

'You filthy dago!' she shouted, shoving him so hard that he toppled backwards into the waters of the pool, accidentally joining in a game of volleyball played with a balloon filled with water, and scoring for a team that didn't know he was playing for their side.

'Manda!' hissed Hugo, who had just watched this little drama. 'You can't call people dagos anymore. It's against the law.'

'So, arrest me. The man was making a pass at me,' she hissed back.

'Really? Are you sure?' asked Mr C-C-C in disbelief.

'And why not? Am I not still an attractive blonde, even if of the mature variety?'

Hugo feigned a coughing fit, stuffed his hankie into his mouth, and went off in search of a quiet corner in which to cry with laughter. Manda was about as inviting as a river full of alligators. He just didn't dare tell her.

The old school party eventually found sanctuary in the ice-cream parlour, as the younger set came in for cornets and ice-lollies between their Banana Daiquiris and Blue Lagoons. They found Douglas Huddlestone-Black in there having a solitary coffee, but he made haste to finish and leave before they had all got seated.

'He's a bit more uppity than he used to be when he visited Mama Headmistress at school. Then, he was all over us like a rash. And he's still quite yummy, isn't he, even after all these years,' said Wuffles, wistfully.

'Maybe we're just not. Still yummy, that is. Maybe he's happily married, or even gay,' suggested Longshanks, who was having trouble getting up on to a high stool at the counter of the parlour, being a shade under five feet tall, and taking size two shoes. She looked strangely like a child suddenly made old, rather than a woman of pensionable age.

'Tell me more about this buying into Parrot Bay?' asked Lady Amanda, who had been feeling rather left out of the main reason for the reunion. She had evidently been asked as a late extra, and was smarting a little at being thus overlooked.

'There are ten properties as yet unsold, and we're going to have a good mooch round them, and the island as a whole, and decide whether we want to invest in retirement in the sun.'

The voices came thick and fast after that. 'My parents are both dead now, and I've finally got probate on Daddy's will.'

'I was thinking of going somewhere where I could guarantee the weather for my poor, aching joints and the sun would be good for my eczema and dry skin.'

'An annuity has just matured, and I think I could just about afford it, what with my private pension as well as the Old Age one.'

'I've got loads stashed away in the bank for a rainy day, but why shouldn't I use it for continuous sunny days instead?'

Every one of them was serious about this, and it certainly gave Lady Amanda food for thought. She got so fed up in the winter with the constant cloud cover in the south of England. It was almost like being under a vast frosted glass dome, and she was beginning to feel like a Victorian specimen for some giant.

Why shouldn't *she* have a place in the sun as well? Obviously, she wouldn't abandon Belchester Towers, but she could certainly do with somewhere warmer in the winter months. And she had a goodly stash of dosh in various accounts and investments.

'The idea is very appealing,' she said in quite a firm voice. 'I don't see why I shouldn't consider joining you in this venture.'

Immediately, three sets of eyes swivelled to stare at her: those of Beauchamp, Enid, and Hugo. Was she out of her mind, or would it be just another one of her adventures or whims? Who knew, but it might be fun trying the idea on for size – as long as they were included in the plan as well.

'Nine Knickerbocker Glories over here, my man,' she trumpeted in the direction of the waiter who was lazily polishing sundae dishes behind the counter. 'And make it snappy!'

Lunch was somewhat less formal than breakfast, as they had finally settled themselves down on a couple of benches on an upper deck where the music was not quite so loud, and had observed a barbecue being fired up for informal eating.

Beauchamp was unanimously, and unfairly, voted to go downstairs, queue, then carry food back upstairs – a total of five trips before everyone was satisfied – and he smouldered as he finally ate his beef burger, covered in ketchup that he fantasised was his employer's blood, and wondered whether this would be the pattern of his whole honeymoon. Instead of being at the beck and call of just two people, maybe he'd find himself enslaved to a much greater number of omnipotent and merciless dictators.

Well, he wouldn't stand for it. This was his and Enid's special time, and they would not be waiting on anyone but themselves. There were five additional lady wrinklies plus one other elderly man in 'their' party, and he was about to be confronted with six more elderly ladies and another crumbly old man. It just would not do.

At this point, the voice of his employer broke into his reveries with some good news and some bad news. She gave him the bad news first. 'I wonder if you would mind going downstairs and getting us all a long cold drink with which to wash down our scratch lunch?'

His expression told her everything she needed to know, and she quickly added the good news. 'There are ample staff for each villa at Parrot Bay, so that you two can have a nice rest.'

Beauchamp was so surprised, he replied before he could think about the words. 'Really? You actually mean that?'

'Are you doubting my word of honour?'

'Of course not, your ladyship. Now, how many orange juices and how many pineapple juices, ladies?'

'Rum punch for me,' came a unanimous chorus of voices. Beauchamp set off, sincerely hoping he would never have to deal with this bunch if they ever got tiddly.

Douglas Huddlestone-Black avoided their company again at dinner, but Beauchamp was aware of some subtle plotting going on, and he feared for the once yummy boy's safety, should this gang decide to pay him back for his unsociability.

There was a lot of whispering, note-passing and sniggering going on that even involved Lady Amanda, and the butler's antennae were fully alert for any mischief afoot. He would definitely have to be on his guard to see that the now elderly man came to no physical harm. Practical jokes were not acceptable from persons as venerable as this, and could have unexpectedly nasty results.

Enid ate mechanically, chewing her fingernails in between courses as a sort of bizarre palate-cleanser, and looking forward to their new cabin which had been allocated to them just prior to dinner. 'What do you think, Beauchamp?' asked Lady A. 'I didn't think the pre-dinner cocktails were up to much – nothing like as good as yours.'

'In my opinion,' began Beauchamp, a smirk of professional superiority on his face, 'I think they are skimping a little on some of the ingredients, and substituting inferior brands for others.'

'They certainly know how to charge for them though, I noticed: and there's a service charge on each one as well, in lieu of tips,' added Hugo.

'I do so dislike that,' Lady Amanda re-joined the conversation. 'When I was younger, one was allowed to leave a tip at the end of a meal or event, and its size depended on how good one considered the service one had received to have been.

This system is so unfair, in that it rewards the mediocre and penalises the really dedicated staff.'

'Then, may I suggest that we still leave or give a suitable tip to anyone from whom we consider we have received exceptional service?' asked Fflageolet, her voice high and piping, giving some credence to her nickname from childhood.

'Jolly good idea, old bean,' agreed the equally tiny figure of Longshanks. 'There's a guy does my cabin who's been an absolute darling so far. Every time I go back to it, he's folded my towels into swans, and he puts chocolate mints and a flower on my bed.'

'Gosh, you are fortunate,' said Wuffles, running her fingers through her dog-like wavy hair. 'I'm lucky if my bottled water's been renewed; and nothing I've used from the mini-bar has been replaced either, and it's just about empty now. I wish they hadn't been so thorough in depriving us of any alcohol we wished to bring on the trip.

'I know we'll get it back in the end, but it really is like being in a police state.'

'They have to do that or they'll lose profits from their sales of drinks,' Lady Amanda pointed out. 'It just means we'll have more to get through when we get there, and Beauchamp can make us some proper cocktails.'

'But...' interrupted Beauchamp.

'Don't worry your head. There are staff where we're staying, and mixing cocktails is all I shall ask you to do. The rest of your time is free to do what you want ... with whomever you want,' she added wickedly.

Both newlyweds blushed.

'And not all of us got so thoroughly frisked.' Horseface's comment brought the conversation to an end.

Chapter Three

The party had not long retired for the night when there was a surreptitious tapping on the door of the suite that Lady Amanda and Hugo were sharing, and she opened the door to reveal Wuffles, wrapped in a towel and holding a bottle of wine and some plastic cups. 'What the heck's this in aid of? It's three minutes past midnight, you know.'

'That's right, and that's why I'm here,' replied Wuffles mysteriously.

'Is that Fflageolet I see creeping down the corridor behind you?'

'Of course it is. Midnight pool party for us old girls. Get your towel and meet us in the pool area. Have you forgotten so soon what we planned at dinner? Everyone who managed to buy or smuggle some booze aboard is bringing it: not quite all of it got confiscated,' replied the towel-clad figure, as other shadowy shapes, similarly wrapped, joined her. 'See you and Hugo in five.'

'Wake up, Hugo!' Lady A trumpeted. 'You've been invited to an exclusive pool party with the old girls' brigade. Get your swimmers on.'

'Whaa ...?' moaned Hugo, sitting up in bed to find his eyes fixed upon Lady A's ample behind, as she pawed her way through the bottom of her side of the closet.

Quickly averting his gaze, he asked her what she thought she was doing. 'Pool party, Hugo. Get your trunks on. You can use the bathroom to change, as I'm going to get into my cozzie in here.'

Hugo harrumphed into one of his clothes drawers and came out holding something that could have been a khaki flag, if such a thing existed, flung it over his shoulder, and disappeared into the tiny bathroom, still making huffing noises of general disapproval.

When he knocked discreetly, and was readmitted to the stateroom proper, he was startled by what confronted him. 'Manda!' he exclaimed. 'Whatever do you think you're wearing?'

'My swimming costume.'

'But it's bright pink.'

'I'd hate to be lost at sea off the island. I thought the colour might help to identify my drowning body being dragged out to the deep.'

'But what is that thing round your waist? It's exactly the same colour. You have got it on over your swimming costume and not under it, haven't you?'

'Of course I have. It's my matching rubber ring. I can't actually swim, you know. Or, at least, I did once, and someone's got it on film, but once I'd had the evidence taken, I decided I didn't like it and would never do it again.'

'So, how do you propose to get out of the cabin door?' asked Hugo biting his lip, when he looked at her width, and that of the door frame.

'Blast. I shall have to let it down a bit,' she snapped, pulling out the plastic bung. Now having time to consider her friend's get-up, she declared,

'Hugo, you've got a hairy chest.'

'I'm allowed to have. I am a man, you know,' he retorted.

'Of course you are, but not one I've ever seen in a state of undress before.'

At this description of his current state of *dishabille*, Hugo put his hands where he would have done were he a footballer in the wall facing a free kick. 'I've got everything necessary covered,' he snapped at her.

'For now,' she replied, enigmatically.

'Whatever do you mean by that?' he asked, transferring his forefingers to cover his naked nipples.

'Those girls can get awfully playful when they've had a few drinks. Oh, stop making faces and follow me, you coward.' Hugo did as he was told, but not without great trepidation.

When they reached the pool deck, she got Hugo to join her at a bench which had a canopy above it for daytime shade, and got him down sufficiently to blow up her ring again. For that, he had to sit on the bench, because his knees still weren't at their best, not having been run-in yet, as they were quite new, and it was with a great whoop of glee that Droopy-Drawers and Horseface came upon them.

'What have we here, then? A little bit of foreplay, or the real thing?' chortled Horseface.

'Hugo is merely blowing up my ring,' replied Lady Amanda with as much dignity as she could muster.

'That's exactly what it looks like, old fruit,'

commented Droopy-Drawers.

'My *rubber* ring, you fools!'

'Any accessories used in the pursuit of love are OK by me.'

'My swimming ring. Crikey, can't a girl wear a rubber ring anymore without someone accusing her of being a pervert?'

'We'll leave you two to it, and we'll see you in the water. By the way, Hugo, nice legs.' Hugo immediately stopped huffing and puffing into the little plastic tube and covered what he could of his legs with his towel.

'Hugo. Pay attention. All the air's coming out of my ring.' The penny finally dropped with Hugo concerning the subject of the girls' mirth, and this final comment reduced him to tears of laughter.

'Put the stopper in for now. I need time to get my breath back,' he managed to say through his gales of ungentlemanly laughter.

'As the actress said to the bishop,' muttered Lady Amanda under her breath, wishing that Enid had been here to carry out this procedure instead of Hugo.

The galumphing and horseplay in the water lasted for about an hour, Hugo returning to the bench in a huff after only twenty minutes, after they had deprived him of his trunks. He had eventually managed to recapture them from between Horseface's teeth, and made himself respectable again before climbing out. Lady Amanda joined him as the hour drew to a close.

'They do play rough, don't they,' he confirmed, his forehead still creased in displeasure.

'They're just a mite lively and excited about

being together again,' his cabin-mate replied.

'Well, I just hope they calm down, or I'm going to spend the bulk of this holiday up a gum-tree, or in this case, hiding up a palm tree. They need a bit of decorum, that's what they need.'

'Never mind. Hugo. I don't think anyone caught sight of your winkle.'

'My what?'

'Nothing.'

'But...'

'Shh, Hugo. I can hear someone down the other side of the deck.'

'What can you hear, Manda?'

'Shh!' she hissed back. 'It's a sort of scraping sound. And, what's that?'

'What's what?'

'I distinctly heard a splash.'

'I didn't.'

'You're going deaf. I'm going to take a look to see what's going on. The others have all cleared off.'

'At this time of night?'

'It sounded sinister to me.' This was all conducted in hushed voices. They were, therefore, very surprised to hear distinct footsteps approaching them from round the corner of the sheltered spot, and to be greeted in normal tones by Douglas Huddlestone-Black.

'Good evening, or should I say, good morning?'

'What are you doing up at this hour?' Lady Amanda challenged him.

'I could say the same about you two. Out for a bit of hanky-panky, are you?'

'Indeed we are not,' replied Lady A, snorting

with a sound like a hippopotamus coming up for air. 'We were with the girls for a midnight swim.'

'A likely tale,' the impertinent, white-haired but still undeniably handsome, man retorted. 'Where are they all now?'

'They've only just left.'

'A likely story. Tell that to the Marines,' he replied with a little smirk.

'And what were you up to, may we ask?' Lady Amanda made so bold.

'Game of cards on the foredeck. Just finished, and thought I'd have a little stroll before turning in,' he replied with an air of insouciance. Hugo kept schtum. Life with his old friend was easier that way.

'Did you hear a sort of dragging sound and a splash just now?' she challenged him, thinking his game of cards was more of the imaginary sort than a real one.

'No, sorry. Did you?'

'Definitely.' Lady A felt determined to get to the bottom of what she had just aurally witnessed.

'Then it was probably one of the crew getting rid of some rubbish over the side – something a bit iffy that he couldn't put into the general trash.'

'Harumph! Highly unlikely, I'd have thought.' she shot back at him.

'Well, as I neither heard nor saw anything. I shall bid you goodnight and, no doubt, see you tomorrow.'

'Definitely suspect,' she muttered, as he strolled off, whistling.

Chapter Four

None of the reunion party rose in time for breakfast the next day, and some sore heads were in evidence but, having missed breakfast, they knew there was twenty-four-hour food available in one of the buffet-style restaurants, and decided to partake of brunch instead. If they didn't pile their plates too high, they might just have room for lunch itself in a couple of hours.

People sat around in the cane chairs stuffing their faces with hot dogs, quarter-pounders, chicken strips, and chips while water dripped from their bodies on to the floor.

'I do wish they wouldn't allow people to come into a dining room straight out of the pool,' sighed Lady Amanda in disapproval. 'If anything I put on my plate tastes of chlorine, I shall make a very noisy and pointed complaint.'

'Oh, quit whining, Manda. I'm starved.' This was Droopy-Drawers, who had not suffered as much from the after-effects of alcohol as some of the others, and was raring to tuck into the various delights displayed for their dining pleasure.

Whatever hangover cures had been employed, their appetites soon returned, and plates were piled high with sausages, tomatoes, scrambled eggs, rolls, and even pancakes and maple syrup, which Lady Amanda had discovered were delicious when eaten with savoury food. Only Hugo remained intimidated by the barely-clad bodies filling the tables, and sat with his back to them as best he could. He said the sight of so much bare flesh made him lose his appetite.

'Have you seen the pecs and the tan on that one over there?' asked Wuffles, like a silly teenager. On receiving a number of disapproving stares, she retorted, 'Well, a girl can dream, can't she? And with a bit of surgery, I could aspire to being a rich plaything with a fit toyboy.'

'A *little* surgery? You'd need so much there'd be a whole pile of leftovers for the surgeon's dog.' pointed out Longshanks, who then snorted into her chips. 'And you'd still look like an old hag.'

'Well, at least I wouldn't need a whole personality transplant so that I sounded like a human being,' Wuffles batted back, before Fflageolet interrupted and told them to quit it.

'I know how you two used to fight at school, but we could do without that sort of childish skirmish on holiday. Now, stop it and call a truce until we get on the plane back home. And if you two decide to move out there, I suggest you live as far apart as possible from each other.'

'Hear hear!' Lady A encouraged Fflageolet. 'It used to be like separating a pair of fighting dogs at school.'

'Looking costs nothing,' mumbled Wuffles, returning to her plate.

'And neither does pure hatred,' said Longshanks, only very, very quietly.

'Oh God, here we go again,' mouthed Lady Amanda, but totally silently.

At lunch, two factions had emerged, being sat this lunchtime at different tables. Hugo was quite upset but, as Lady Amanda pointed out to him, they had kept in touch all these years, and those two had always been like that. Wuffles and Long-shanks were separated by the width of the room, and accompanied by Droopy-Drawers had also managed to capture Douglas Huddlestone-Black for their table.

Horseface and Fflageolet sat with her and Hugo, so there was an even split. Beauchamp and Enid had not shown up for the meal and, either they had had room service, dined at a different time, or given lunch a complete miss. Still, it was their honeymoon after all, and Lady Amanda rather hoped they'd get that sort of thing out of their systems on the way over, so that Beauchamp could concentrate on making cocktails for the whole party once they were ensconced in their temporary island homes.

They left the dining table about half-past one, all but Lady Amanda and Hugo going off to their cabins for a siesta after their alcohol-fuelled very late night. The pair still standing had not indulged much in the old drinky-poos; therefore Hugo was dragged off to play deck games, as the rest of the ship was just waking up after its turn-in between four and six a.m.

They started with shuffleboard, which was going fine until Hugo managed to shuffle his puck into a group of young girls who were wearing the nearest thing to nothing in the bikini department, and they decided to make a fuss of him. It took Lady Amanda ten minutes to disentangle him, and a

42

further fifteen for him to stop blushing. 'Three of them pinched my bottom, Manda, and another one – I didn't see which – actually cupped my, er, um, meat and two, er, veg, in one of her hands,' he squeaked, going pink again.

'That's a bit rum, getting your winkle fondled by a young girl,' retorted Lady A before she could think, then added, 'I'll just get us something to perk us up a bit.' She was suddenly embarrassed for her shy old friend, and took herself off to the pool bar, where she ordered two large brightly coloured cups of rum punch.

On her return, Hugo grabbed his gratefully, and gulped most of it down. 'I needed that!' he sighed, handing it back to her for a refill.

'What did your last slave die of?' she replied, then added, 'Why don't you take off your tie, or at least put on a T-shirt and a pair of shorts? There's no need for such a formal outfit aboard.' He was, even at sea, wearing a suit, for all the world like he was in an office or at a meeting!

'I haven't got anything else,' he retorted, to her retreating back. 'I've never been anywhere warm before.'

After he had drunk his second large cocktail, Lady Amanda dragged him off to the ship's shop and ordered him to select half a dozen T-shirts and a similar number of pairs of shorts, plus a couple of pairs of flip-flops. Instead of making the fuss that she had expected, he became girlishly giggly as he held up garment after garment, actually filling a large bag with his purchases, which Lady A returned to their stateroom before dragging him off to try deck quoits.

43

He now wore a Hawaiian-style short-sleeved shirt, a floppy white hat that would have graced any donkey, and a pair of turquoise knee-length shorts. On his feet were flip-flops, which he had begun to complain about as soon as he had tried walking in them. 'They're impossible, Manda. How do I get them to stay on? Glue?'

'Just curl your toes, and the thong thingy between your toes should help.'

'What thong thingy between what toes?'

Lady Amanda looked down, and her mouth fell open. 'I simply do not believe you, Hugo. That rubber thong goes between your big toe and the one next to it. I've never in my life met anyone who tried to wear flip-flops sideways. You're a one-off, you are, getting in such a flip-flop flap.'

She adjusted his footwear, and he had to admit that he could walk again, and that they were really most comfortable. 'Never tried anything like it in my life,' he almost sang. 'I feel so free.'

Approaching the area for deck quoits, Lady Amanda handed him a rope quoit, pointed in the right direction, and told him to feel free to start the game anytime he felt like it. With this, she threw her first rope ring with exquisite accuracy. Hugo threw his overboard.

She gave him another one, explained about how to get the aim right, flung her own, and told him to try again. This time his quoit hit a trayful of drinks that a pool waiter was just delivering to a gaggle of young women; happily not the ones who had recently groped her opponent.

'I hope he doesn't expect a tip for that,' said Hugo, and took another quoit from Lady A.

For the third time, Lady A's throw was spot on. This time, Hugo's went through an open doorway, and they could hear it bouncing down a flight of metal stairs. There was a crash and a scream, and a shattering of glass, then silence. 'Let's get out of here, Hugo. I do believe you've bowled someone off their feet, and it's time we weren't here. Are you squiffy after just two rum punches?'

Hugo smiled a smile that suggested that a village, somewhere, was missing its idiot, and they left the deck to get a cup of coffee in the café. Perhaps it would help him sober up.

That evening they decided to try out the dancing, leaving the restaurant around nine and heading towards the music. It would certainly not be Viennese waltzes and foxtrots from the sound of it, but they were determined to have a go, just because they were there.

It was so crowded that they had to snake their way between gyrating bodies exuding hormones and sweat in equal proportions. Hugo was particularly clumsy at this, and his progress was marked by cries of 'ow' and 'ouch' and 'mind out' – or at least a version of that last one.

He was thoroughly hot and bothered by the time he reached the bar, and he clutched on to it as a drowning man might grasp the side of a lifeboat. 'I don't like it in here, Manda,' he yelled above the booming music. Lady A was thinking exactly the same thing herself, when a young female in a dress that left very little to the imagination caught him from behind, whirled him round and, clasping her hands about his neck, began to

45

sway close against his body.

Hugo gave a strangled scream and tried to untangle himself, but his partner was determined to fulfil the dare her mate had issued. Pushing her sweating face against his, her lips began to move against his lips in the motion of a passionate kiss, and Hugo found that he couldn't breathe, as her face was also blocking his nose. When she tried to insinuate her tongue between his tightly closed lips, he lost his temper and panicked at the same time.

Lifting a foot, he stamped on one of her stiletto-clad feet as hard as he could – not very gentlemanly, but he was suffocating under the suction of her face on his. He followed this up with a quick kick on the shin. That broke her hold, and he came up for air, already turning to make an escape from his captor. But he needn't have bothered; or rather, it was just as well that he did, for she stood stock still, bent forward slightly, and vomited on exactly the spot on which he had been standing.

As he approached the bar, Lady Amanda grabbed his arm and said, 'Come on, Hugo. This is no place for us,' and steered him towards the exit. They had to undergo the same struggle through the throng of people to escape, but they eventually made it, leaving behind them an even larger number of people bemoaning the fact that someone had trodden on their toes. 'We shall not be returning to that particular venue,' Lady A announced as they reached the safety of the corridor that led to the atrium. 'I'm glad I'm not young, if one has to behave like that.'

'We were young once, but I believe we had

much better manners,' retorted Hugo, heaving a huge sigh of relief to be safe again, and away from that nearly-nude female octopus. 'I've never been so frightened in my life.'

That night, Hugo woke several times with a loud whimpering noise, from his nightmares about the unspeakable assault which had been perpetrated upon his person earlier.

The cruise finally came to an end, and before they knew it, their cases had been put on the dock, and they were waiting to disembark, with about two thousand other cruisers, who were only going to spend the day on the island. The view was terrific. There were golden beaches, there was a turquoise lagoon. To their left was what they were to learn was the jewellery quarter, and to the left of that, in the distance, a gathering of rather exclusive-looking villas. The backdrop was tropical, a positive jungle of palm trees and other exotic growth through which, to the right, peeped the summit of a mountain.

And there, on the dockside, were the rest of the members of the school reunion party, waving Union Jacks and shouting their heads off.

'May we disembark, please?' enquired Lady Amanda, in her most imperial voice.

'You've gotta wait till the buses show up,' replied a rather scruffy crew member, trying to issue her with a paper sticker.

'Don't you dare try to touch that part of my body,' she squealed, as his hand approached her right breast. 'We are not going on a coach trip. We are disembarking here for a holiday with the island's owners' – not quite technically accurate, but it sounded good.

'Oo-er, 'oity-toity, missus. Pardon me breathing,' was the only reply she received, as he waved the whole party of old girls, Douglas Huddlestone-Black included, through the rope that had been across the gangplank, and let them go with a sarcastic smile and an ironic wave – at least, that's what Lady Amanda said they were, as she bustled indignantly down the gangplank, trying her hardest not to lose her balance on the steep gradient. She had managed, by sheer willpower, to misinterpret the one-fingered gesture that the ill-mannered seaman had made at them.

Chapter Five

Standing next to their luggage, they were engulfed in a party of colourfully dressed women and one man. Douglas Huddlestone-Black, after a clipped 'Hello,' went off on his own, heading west. Red, white, blue, pink, purple, turquoise, gold, yellow: the proliferation of colours was rather like being landed on by a flock of huge, noisy parrots.

'Yoohoo, Horseface!'

'Coo-ee, Sniffy. Got yer toyboy in tow then?'

'You're an hour late. We've already had to take a break for a long, cool drink.'

'Tiddly-pom, Droopy-Drawers.'

Lady Amanda shouted loudly for silence, then began the introductions, for the benefit of Hugo and Mr and Mrs Beauchamp. 'We'll start with these two. Beauchamp is my butler-cum-general factotum, Enid is an old friend and his new wife...'

At this, cat-calls issued from the welcome party, 'and this is my very old friend Hugo, whom some of you may have met before when you stayed with me in the holidays, all those centuries ago.' The thought that they may have come across Beauchamp during these visits did not even occur to her, as none of her friends ever spared a glance for servants, and he would have been very young – maybe just a fill-in boot boy, and she rather felt that both she and Beauchamp would be the better for her not announcing that he was her illegitimate half-brother. Lady Amanda then passed the introductions baton over to Windy.

'For the purposes of these three,' began Windy Bartholomew, 'may I introduce Butterfingers Bartholomew' – a chunky woman with a startlingly lilac-coloured rinse in her hair – 'Hefferlump Leclerc' – a fat woman with very short white hair – 'Snotty Nosegay' – a wisp of a woman with red eyes, sneezing into a handkerchief that looked as if it were long overdue for a change – 'Hopalong Cassidy: yes, ha ha everyone' – a tall, broadly-built woman with long grey-white hair in a plait – 'Eeyore Montrose' – here, she indicated a woman with a lugubrious face – 'And finally, me, Windy Winterbottom' – the very curvaceous woman dressed in the height of tropical fashion wiggled her fingers at them, then continued.

'Not forgetting my ever-loving partner, Beep-Beep Morris, the light of my life,' she crooned. 'And don't worry if you're newcomers to this group, I have a list at home waiting for you, with everyone's names on, and the number of the villa in which they'll be staying. We'll soon all be the best of friends again, or even for the first time.'

Distinguishable from the crowd of elderly ladies, two scowled at each other, and there was certainly no love lost between them. They had never got on, Longshanks and Wuffles.

'Where's Douglas?' asked Wuffles, shaking her head to dispel the feeling of dislike that had just washed over her. 'He just sort of sloped off on his own, and we hardly saw him aboard ship.'

'He'll just have made for his usual villa. He's not all that sociable until he gets into the swing of island life again,' replied Windy, smiling round at all the familiar faces about her.

'Probably upset by losing his cabin steward like that,' put in Horseface, as explanation.

'What happened to his cabin steward, then?' Suddenly Lady A was all ears. Was this what she and Hugo had heard happening after the midnight swim?

'He just disappeared off the ship. Everyone was talking about it. I think it was the afternoon you and Hugo went off to play deck games. It was assumed that he'd somehow gone overboard, or somehow jumped ship. Douglas was very upset about it.'

'I'll bet he was,' said Lady Amanda, her face thoughtful, her head full of that night, when she had hear the sound of what could have been a body being dragged, followed by a splash, and the sudden appearance of Douglas Huddlestone-Black, apparently just taking a casual early-hours

50

stroll around the deck.

She would keep her mouth shut for now, as Hugo had been a little too hard of hearing to notice it – he said he had water in his ears, but she didn't believe him – and just see if anything else occurred that might shed light on this peculiar incident of what the gay dog did in the night. And she must stop using that expression: it meant something totally different now, or so people told her.

For Your Information:
Numbers

1 – Horseface and Fflageolet – FOR SALE
3 – FOR SALE
5 – Adonis – FOR SALE
7 – Wuffles, Droopy-Drawers, and Longshanks – FOR SALE
9 – Hefferlump – The Palms
11 – Butterfingers – Tropical Hideaway
12A – Snotty – Lagoon View
15 – Sniffy and Hugo – FOR SALE
16 – Windy and Beep-Beep – Cocktails

Opposite

2 – Hopalong – Coconut Corner
4 – FOR SALE
6 – FOR SALE
8 – Beauchamp and Enid – FOR SALE
10 – FOR SALE
12– FOR SALE
14 – Eeyore – West Indies Retreat

NB: As there is no 13, please note that 16 is on the odd numbers side

The above information was presented to all those staying, for their convenience, to avoid confusion as to who was staying where, and with whom – and, of course, to highlight which of the properties were currently available for purchase. It was all neatly set out on a sheet of A4 which Windy had printed for them, and from which she had great hopes of some more properties being sold.

The whole development had been expensive to build, and it would not be until they were all sold that she and Beep-Beep would reap the full reward for their entrepreneurial spirit. Those already living there had been allotted the title to their villas by dint of their initial investment in the business proposition, and Windy bemoaned the fact that they had not, yet, yielded a bean, what with building costs and the original purchase of the land. Windy never even blushed as she made this public declaration of (comparative) poverty.

As the whole group perused this complicated list of house numbers and nicknames, Longshanks suddenly sighed and said, 'I don't know how I'm going to face my unpacking. I do so wish I had that lovely cabin steward from the boat. Horseface told you he disappeared, didn't she? I don't know whether he was assigned to other duties, but I got a painfully shy woman next, who blushed if I even looked at her, and she wasn't a patch on my dear old Sam with his towel swans. Did he do any of you, too?'

There was a chorus of 'no's, then Fflageolet

piped up with, 'I'm fairly sure he did Adonis' cabin as well. He said something about a Sam, and said he thought it was scandalous that all the Filipinos had been given English names to make it easier for the passengers. He was sure we could have managed to use their real names, just to reserve a bit of dignity for them in their menial work.'

'That's very interesting,' muttered Lady Amanda, and was given furiously to think. Back to her mind came again the sound of dragging, the splash, then, a few seconds later, Huddlestone-Black appearing round the corner on the deck the night they had gone for a midnight swim. Every time she thought about this, she became more and more convinced that their lovely Adonis had done for his steward. Was there dirty work afoot here? Was their darling Douglas really hiding a sinister side? She was beginning to feel quite sure of it, and this was the second time the subject had been raised since they had landed, albeit by different people.

She must speak to Beauchamp later, if she could drag him away from Enid. At this thought, she saw, in her mind's eye, a crowbar, and decided that she would have to find a way to entice him away from his newly made-up marital bed, just for a consultation. Then she could try to explain her fears to Hugo. The privacy of their own villa would at least allow her to raise her voice without anyone else hearing. In her opinion, there were dark deeds afoot, and nothing would persuade her otherwise.

Her reverie was broken by the penetrating voice of Windy who, clapping her hands loudly, called, 'Attention everyone, please. Your luggage will

53

arrive any minute on the island bus. Staff will deliver it to your quarters, then we shall get on board and go on an island tour so that you can fully appreciate the beauties of Caribbaya.

'When we have done that we'll take a trip to Old Uncle Obediah's Rum Keg Landing Beach Bar, timed for when the cruise ship has to leave, so that there is not too much of a crowd and, finally, we shall finish up at the Parakeet Club. All your belongings will be safely stored while we are gone, and we can get back here for a leisurely nightcap before retiring for the night. I trust that sounds agreeable to all of you?'

There was a muttering of agreement and a smattering of applause, as she received universal approval, and it was only a minute or so later when they heard the frantic hooting of a horn, and an elderly bus bucketed along the road towards them with a definite list to starboard, as it drew up before them.

'Ah put de valises on de left,' a deep voice called through the open driver's window, and they all made the acquaintance of Winstone Churchill, the unforgettably-named bus driver. 'When you lovely ladies load yourselves on, make sure you load de weight evenly between both sides, oderwise dis ole jalopy sways like an ole boat on de rollin' waves.'

'Hi there, Winstone. You all ready for this tour?' called Windy.

'I's as ready as I's ever goin' t' be. I've checked de mike's workin', and I's ready to roll when you are, Miz Wendy. Ah'll just unload de baggage.'

'Come along, girls and boys: let's go and check out this beautiful island,' Windy exhorted them, and shepherded them on to the dilapidated vehicle. 'We're having a few events throughout the island to try to raise funds towards a new bus.

'We're organising themed events in the jewellery district, the market, the township, and by the lagoon over the next couple of months. And if Beep-Beep and I make any sales in the near future, we shall make a suitably sizeable donation to the funds. Now, everybody ready? Then, off we go. Hi ho, Winstone,' tootled Windy. Winstone was in his seat again, having left the luggage for the villa staff to sort out and deliver, as it was all labelled, and with a large and smoky backfire they were off.

The suspension of the bus produced a state which was rather like being at sea in a very small craft, as it rolled with the punches of the potholes in the road, but soon they were skirting the coast heading west. It wasn't long before Windy pointed out two watering holes within walking distance of their accommodation: namely Old Uncle Obediah's Rum Keg Landing Beach Bar, which was actually on the sands, and the Lizard Lounge, a cocktail bar which had got its name, not because of its predatory male patrons, but because of its saurian visitors.

Rounding a headland, heading north-east now, they arrived at the outskirts of a colourful market, bursting with the smells of ripe fruit and cooking meats and vegetables. This was where a lot of the indigenous islanders sold their wares, and even those that worked for households in Parrot Bay, or on the land, lived just a short way away in the township, which was on the northern coast.

The township was a ramshackle gathering of wooden buildings in myriad colours and assorted states of repair, but was memorable for its atmosphere of friendliness, all those out on the streets waving to Winstone and his passengers as they passed through, and small children, almost naked in the tropical weather, running after the dilapidated old vehicle, laughing and shouting.

He then coaxed the rickety old bus inland, through a forest road which then almost turned back on itself to take them to the foot of the mountain, round which a road ran. Apparently this was a fairly new route, as the coves on the far side of it used to be accessible only from the sea, and were said to be the site of a lot of smuggling in the past.

The bus then headed for the buildings of the cruise terminal, driving slowly towards what was known as the jewellery district. Although there were a few places that sold souvenirs and food, the shops were mainly full of gold, silver and precious stones, supplemented by fabulous quality (and price) clocks and watches.

This was the main tourist trap, apart from the market, to which Winstone ran regular trips for the day visitors and, as there was no tourist accommodation on the island, made the bulk of its money when the ships docked for the day. Thus, its employees had limited working hours, giving them more freedom than those usually employed in retail establishments, although a ship mooring overnight sometimes gave them very long hours.

Winstone let them off at a bronze statue of a figure he told them was Admiral Lord Horatio

Nelson, although no one could actually see any resemblance, but proving that the island had once been under the care and administration of the British government, and instructed them to meet him back there in one hour exactly. 'Latecomers will find theirselves walkin' home,' he announced, 'I's still got ma normal routes to cover when I's not chauffeurin' around dis bunch o' fine ladies ... and gents.' He looked at Hugo with big, brown, apologetic eyes at this near omission. He waved them off imperiously as he drove away in a cloud of smoke and a salute of back-fires. Beauchamp and Enid, and Douglas Huddlestone-Black, were conspicuous by their absence.

Lady Amanda took Hugo's proffered arm, and they began to stroll through the thronging crowd of cruisers on their one-day Caribbayan sprees, with a feeling of superiority. They must have arrived early, as Windy had expected all these shoppers to have left by the time they arrived, but at least it allowed Lady Amanda to swank around as one of the few people who were actually sleeping on the island, instead of just making a lightning visit.

All the shops had signs which informed them that the establishments were open late on Friday evenings exclusively for local residents – provided there was no craft in port offering greater potential to snag the unwary.

Window shopping was a mouthwatering experience in Lady A's opinion – she did love her jewellery – but it was only about twenty minutes before Hugo began to complain about his feet and knees. 'Let's go and find somewhere to sit down,' he whined, sounding just like a petulant child.

'Over there.' pointed Lady A, espying a rather upmarket coffee shop. 'We'll go in there and have a jolt of caffeine. I feel I could do with one.'

Once inside, Hugo flopped into a chair with gratitude, while Lady Muck went to the counter to solicit immediate waitress service. When she returned with a pretty local girl clutching two menus, Hugo pointed excitedly, through the window towards a jeweller's opposite. 'You'll never guess who I've just seen,' he said, excitedly.

'Hush, dear. We need to give this charming waitress our orders.'

'Not now. Listen…'

'Just two coffees, please, dear. Nothing fancy. Just Americanos.' Turning to sit down, Lady A said impatiently. 'What on earth are you wittering on about now, Hugo, and why couldn't it wait?'

Hugo bounced in his seat and pointed again. 'There he is, coming out now, and doesn't he look furtive. And he's dressed very casually – almost scruffy. See, he's putting on a hat and pulling down the brim.'

Lady Amanda's eyes followed Hugo's gesturing finger and saw a familiar shape exiting a tres-snob jewellery establishment and slithering down a narrow alleyway, as if he had no desire to be seen or recognised. 'I know who that is, but he didn't come on the bus with us, did he? And why was he wearing those extraordinary clothes. If you hadn't pointed him out I would never have recognised him. Whatever is he up to?'

'And why didn't he just come on the bus with us?' asked Hugo, equally mystified. That figure had definitely been Douglas Huddlestone-Black, and acting very shiftily.

'I have no idea, Hugo, but I intend to find out,' replied Lady Amanda, a familiar gleam taking residence in her eyes. 'We've run into a tasty little mystery here, and I, for one, intend to get to the bottom of it.'

The weather too hot for further conversation, they spent the rest of their free time sipping their huge coffees and fanning their faces with the menus.

When they got back on the rickety old bus, Hugo was feeling a little heat-exhausted, and leaned on what appeared to be an arm rest at the edge of his seat on the aisle side, Lady Amanda having, naturally, claimed the window seat. With a 'whoof' of surprise, down went the arm, and Hugo with it, he having, unfortunately, leant his full weight on it, and he was left with his upper body dangling, with no hope of ever being able to right himself without assistance.

'You people never been on a Caribbean bus before?' screeched Winstone, trundling purposefully down the aisle towards the collapsed marionette figure of Mr C-C-C.

'No. Why?' asked Lady Amanda, genuinely wondering what the man meant.

'Dat don't be no armrest, lady. Dat be one of the oder seats for when de bus get crowded.' Here, he gave Hugo a mighty heave and restored his upright position. 'Look!' he continued, pulling down 'armrests' from the two seats either side of the aisle in front. 'Dey be de seats for de overflow, see?'

They saw. 'And,' their determined island guide

went on, 'dere ain't no timetable, neither. It's not like when I's doin' da chaufferin'. De bus go when de bus is full, and dat means when all de seats is taken, not just de ones beside de aisle.'

'So, how does anyone get anywhere on time?' asked Hugo in a concerned voice.

'Dey don't. Dis is de Caribbean, and you just chill out and get dere when de bus is good and full. See?' With a shrug of his shoulders, he returned to the driver's seat, caught up his microphone and announced, 'Ladies and gentlemen, we be goin' to da lagoon now, where a picnic will be laid out, ready for you. Feel free to shed your inhibitions and your clothes, and take a swim in de blue, warm waters.'

'Buggered if I'm going to do that!'

Hugo could hardly believe his ears. Lady Amanda had actually used a swear word. 'Whatever's got into you, Manda?' he asked.

'That dirty-minded old bus driver just wants to see all us girls in the buff,' she replied, tartly.

'If he does, he's either a pervert, or he really needs his eyes tested.' Ignoring the glare he got for this comment, Hugo added, 'Have you actually looked at some of these old girls? They're enough to turn a man's stomach, if imagined naked. Yuk! No, no, I daren't even try to think about it.'

'That's not very gentlemanly, Hugo.'

'And what's beneath their clothes isn't very ladylike. I'm sure it would look like a mass meeting of hippos and over-sized stick insects, all in need of a damned good ironing.'

'And what about you in swimmers?'

'I think I'd be on the hippos' team,' he replied,

in a cool voice.

'And what about me?'

'Definitely on the side of the angels,' he replied smoothly, knowing full well on which side his bread was buttered.

After a lazy few hours in the shade of the palms on the sandy shores of the lagoon, having decided to give the beach bar a miss, they travelled, pink and content, to the Parakeet Club, just a short way along the road back to Parrot Bay. 'They have a nightly barbecue there,' explained Windy. 'They start it small, and if people turn up, they just put extra food on. There are always plenty of sweet potatoes and fruit to fill up with.'

The Parakeet Club certainly woke them out of their somnolence. A group of men from the township played reggae here for pleasure and free drinks, and there was also a congo drummer. The walls were patterned with paper that showed dense jungle foliage, and toy monkeys swung from the rafters. The barbecue was outside at the back, from which tantalising and mouth-watering smells wafted, making newly-arrived mouths water, although it was not too long since they had picnicked.

Large glass jugs tinkling with ice-cubes and filled with tropical punch were laid on two enormous tables waiting for them, and soon they were ushered out to the back of the building to load plates with meat, plantains, and the local rice dish. Sweet potatoes were squeezed on to plates already overloaded with food, and the group of old school chums reassembled back inside.

'I say, it's just like the days when we went on a school trip, isn't it?' asked Horseface of everyone. 'We always had our packed lunches eaten before the coach left the school grounds, and then had to buy something to eat when we got where we were going. We were always eating in those days, for we had a good supper when we got back to school, and the breakfasts weren't mean either.'

'And some always ate more than their fair share,' was heard, the voice unidentified, but both Windy, who was curvaceous, and Butterfingers and Hefferlump, who were more on the chunky side of chubby, blushed and looked around to see who had made such an unkind remark, and for a while there was an uncomfortable atmosphere.

After a few glasses from the constantly refilled jugs, however, the bonhomie flowed as smoothly as the tropical punch, and good humour was soon restored.

'And what did our lovely Adonis do today?' asked Lady A, with a sly smile on her face. 'I didn't see him on the bus.'

'He said he'd been working so hard that he just wanted to chill out this afternoon – doze in a hammock out in the back garden on the veranda. He said he'd probably just catch an early night and see us, maybe, tomorrow,' Windy informed them.

'How interesting.' Lady Amanda was really intrigued now. She and Hugo must have been the only two people who caught sight of him as he furtively snuck out of that classy jeweller's shop. Whatever could he have been up to? And why had he lied to Windy about what he intended to do? She couldn't think of any connection with the disappearance of a cabin steward from the cruise ship: and that would have long sailed by now, so that, as they say, was that.

Most of the old girls were gorging themselves on lobster, crab, and shrimp, when the proprietor, an ex-pat by the name of Albert Ross, grabbed a microphone and asked them to give a big, warm, Caribbayan welcome to their special guest tonight, Doctor Congo, who would now drum for their entertainment.

'Don't see how drumming can be entertainment,' muttered Lady A into Windy's ear, then asked, 'Who's he, anyway: that chap with the mike?'

'That's our Albie. Mr Ross if you're being formal. He opened this place about a year ago, but it's not doing as well as it should do, because it's just a bit too far away from the cruise terminal, and the island only has the one bus which does round tours rather than 'Come to the Parakeet Club' tours.

'He's been so unlucky. He had a bar in London which was struck by lightning and burnt down. Then, when he'd got the insurance money, he opened a place on the south coast, but that got flooded two years in a row, and he eventually couldn't afford his premiums, so he came out here to make a fresh start, and now this place seems to be on the wane.'

'I suppose it would really help him if you sold all your properties. That should give his business a boost, to have them all occupied with retired people who like to have a good time,' Lady

Amanda suggested.

'Oh, it would, and we hope we shall all be able to patronise this establishment during your stay here – support your local enterprise, sort of thing.' Windy was smiling with her mouth, but her eyes looked anxious, only for them to resolve themselves into relief when Lady Amanda said she thought they would come here often for the food and the entertainment.

At that point, Dr Congo gave himself a fabulous introduction and a big hand, and proceeded to bash the living daylights out of a series of tall drums that stood in front of him and, for a while, no one could hear themselves think, let alone speak.

By the time he finished, to rapturous applause, the effects of the insidious drink in the jugs had begun to take effect, and a feeling of relaxed contentment was noticeable round the two large tables. Albie Ross came over with two more re-filled jugs and took the old ones away, and Hugo had to be roused from a doze into which he had fallen the minute the applause for the drummer had died away.

Shaking his head to rouse his senses, he said, 'I think I need to get back and go to bed. How's everyone else?'

'Winstone?' called Windy, in a stentorian voice, which had helped her no end on the lacrosse field. 'Do you think you could take Hugo home? He's in number fifteen. His clothes should have been put away by now, so he should be able to get ready for bed without too much hassle.'

Everyone else had elected to stay on, and it was

with gratitude that Hugo went off alone in the bus with Winstone, towards his bed and oblivion. He wasn't one who could party like the others. He needed his beauty sleep, otherwise he might end up looking even worse than he thought he already did – just one big wrinkle.

Hugo stirred in his sleep, sometime afterwards, when the bus entered the development, reverberating with a full-volume Bob Marley song accompanied by the voices of everyone aboard. The old chums had had a proper Caribbayan party. And they'd know about it in the morning.

Chapter Six

The only one up with the lark the next morning was Hugo, who found himself totally alone in the kitchen trying to find his way around the cupboards to gather together the few bits and pieces he would need to make a light breakfast.

He had no sooner got his head into the back of a cupboard under the work surface than a cheery Caribbean voice behind him greeted him with, 'Good mornin', sir. Don't you go fussin' yourself round those old cupboards. I's here to do that for you.

'M'name's Maria – housemaid to Miz Winterbottom. She thought you could do with a li'l help with the domestics, an' she sent me over to help.'

Hugo's reply was lost in his yell as he tried to straighten up, taken by surprise as he had been, and hitting his head on the inside top of the cupboard.

'Come here an' let me look at dat. How you manage to hit your head I don' know. You's Mr Hugo, right?'

'Right, Maria. I'm rather afraid you startled me, but your help would be greatly appreciated. I don't know where anything is: I'm afraid I'm a hopeless case when it comes to kitchens,' he replied, submitting to bending his head and having the new arrival ruffle through his hair as if she were a monkey grooming one of her troop.

'No blood, so you's alright, Mr Hugo. Now, what can I get you? Some mango and melon? An omelette? Some pancakes and maple syrup? You tell me, I do you whatever you want.'

'Gosh, what an exotic choice. I ... I really can't make up my mind, Maria.'

'Den sit yourself down at de table an' I'll choose for you,' she chirruped.

Hugo settled himself down at the table in the vast tiled kitchen/breakfast room and mentally rubbed his hands together. He was enjoying this holiday immensely, and believed it could only get better. His joints didn't ache anywhere near as much as they did in England, and his skin was constantly warm, as a reminder of what the sun was doing to his pale outer self.

'How are Windy and, er, Beep-Beep' – he felt a right 'nana using such a silly nickname – 'going to manage without you while we're here?' he asked, more out of politeness than actual concern.

'Oh, she and de massa can manage well on dere own. Dey sent all four of us off to villas while dey

66

got all you guests, just so you don't have to do de housework,' she explained.

Hugo had a quick mental count. 'Surely we're occupying five villas?' He was sure he wasn't mistaken.

'Dat Mr Huddlestone-Black don't want no help whenever he's here. He never let anyone into de place he stays in.'

'How extraordinary,' exclaimed Hugo, thinking of how furtive and secretive the chap had been in avoiding the company of all the old chums on the ship, and how he had scooted off on his own as soon as they had set foot on the island.

He was jolted from this reverie by the hooting of his companion, who came galumphing down the stairs calling, 'Are you up already, Hugo? Ooh, my thumping head. I think I'd better lay off the coconut rum. I must say, I'm starving though, even if I do have what is commonly known as a hangover, and…'

She ground to a halt as she saw the dusky bulk of Maria chopping fruit at the counter. 'May I introduce you to Maria, your friend Windy's housemaid, who has been sent to look after us during our stay here. Maria, this is Lady Amanda Golightly.'

Lady Amanda padded across to shake hands, but before she could reach Maria, the maid had dropped her a deep curtsy. 'I never thought to meet me a real English Lady. Very happy to serve you, Your Majesty,' she said, with a deep-throated chuckle of sheer pleasure.

'Oh, just call me Manda … or, at least, Lady Amanda,' requested that regal figure, quickly changing her mind about complete informality with a servant. Lady Amanda was what was required, and that's what she ought to be called to give her her full ... well, her full something or other, which befitted her station in life.

'Good morning Lady Amanda,' trilled Maria, returning to her slicing and chopping. 'May I have the honour of providing you with some breakfast?'

'Absolutely, my dear. I could eat a scabby donkey.'

After a thoughtful moment, Maria retorted with, 'Well, dat may be an English delicacy, and I ain't got none here, but I can offer you tropical fruit, omelette, or pancakes and syrup. Which would you prefer?'

'All of them!' decided Lady A greedily, and her mouth began to water at the thought of such an exotic and varied breakfast.

'And I'll put a little Caribbayan hot sauce in your omelettes, to really give you a flavour of de island,' their erstwhile cook concluded.

Within a couple of minutes they were sharing a platter of mixed tropical fruits, all of them ripe and still sun-warmed.

'Siz goo', innit?' mumbled Lady A, juice running off her chin and on to her plate.

'What was that, Manda? Didn't quite catch what you said.'

'I said, "This is good, isn't it?"' she clarified, using her napkin to mop not only her chin but her elbows as well.

'Exceptionally,' replied Hugo, unintentionally dribbling pineapple juice into the coffee which had just been placed before him. 'Never had fruit like it in my life before.'

Maria came across and replaced his fruity cup with a fresh one, before returning with two steaming omelettes for their enjoyment. 'Eat up!' she exhorted them. 'You two look like you used to eatin' good, so ole Maria here is goin' to keep it dat way, while you is under her care.'

Luckily, neither of the diners had ears for this comment, which in England might have been taken for a slur on one's figure, but in the Caribbean was a compliment to your status and hearty lifestyle. And to be honest, Maria looked like she 'ate good' as well – but then she did work for Windy and Beep-Beep, and they wouldn't get full value for money out of a constantly hungry maid.

The hot sauce in the omelette was a real surprise, in that it was very palatable and less scorching to the mouth than they had expected. What Maria hadn't told them about was its unique quality of burning more on the way out, than on the way in, but they'd find that out for themselves during the next twenty-four hours.

The pancakes also went down a treat, but they had slowed down by then, and by the time the last one had disappeared down Lady A's throat, they were both bloated but content. Then the phone rang.

'Hello, Sniffy. Windy here. Can you meet me out front? Cat fight at number one. Spit-spot!'

Lady Amanda headed purposefully towards the door. There was always the chance of some serious fall-outs between the girls. Why should life be any different from when they were at school, just because they were now all elderly? Windy had been head girl, and Lady Amanda supposed she too had been summoned because she had been ink monitor in their early years there, and a prefect towards the end of their school careers.

Windy was already standing out in the road, her make-up immaculate and wearing spangled flip-flops, a white hat, and the most blinding full-length orange and pink kaftan. 'Hi ho, Sniffy. Time for the law to intervene,' she tootled, and marched down towards the first house on the other side of the development walking at such a pace that Lady Amanda had a hard task to make her short and rather chubby legs move fast enough to keep up.

'What,' puff puff, 'happened?' Huff huff. 'What started,' suck blow, 'this particular fight?' she asked, fighting to get her breath.

'Well, you remember that Fflageolet's other name at school was Ffion the Ffilcher? She had that year or two when she turned into a mad klep-tomaniac? It seems she might be at it again. Horseface called and said that Fflageolet had stolen her diamond tennis bracelet, and wouldn't give it back, let alone own up to taking it. The whole thing got physical when Horseface was still on the phone to me.'

By now they had reached the first villa, and the sound of angry curses and screams could be heard from within. Windy marched straight in and followed the row upstairs to the landing, where Fflageolet stood on tiptoe to reach a hand-ful of Horseface's hair, and Horseface had a hand round her housemate's throat.

'Quit it, girls! *Maintenant!*' yelled Windy, who had always had a gob on her, and the action froze mid-curse. 'Take your hands off each other and tell me, sensibly and quietly, what the bloody hell is going on here? Is this the way to act at an old school reunion? Whatever would Mrs Huddlestone-Black have said if she'd caught you like this?'

The name of their former formidable headmistress had a sobering effect on both combatants, and they hung their heads in shame. 'Now, what in the name of all that's holy has happened here?' asked Windy in a slightly quieter but still stern tone of voice.

'She stole my tennis bracelet,' hissed Horseface, malignantly. 'It's just like before, at school.'

'Didn't,' came back a harsh and furious reply. 'I never touched her filthy tennis bracelet.'

'Did.'

'Didn't.'

'Did.'

'Shut up!' roared Windy. 'Both of you. Now, let's go downstairs. I want you in separate rooms to tell your stories, then we're going to sort this out one way or another. Don't start!' she roared, as Fflageolet opened her mouth to protest again. 'Downstairs. Now. Both of you.'

Taking the lead herself, she told Lady Amanda to go behind to act as a sort of sheepdog, in case one of them tried to make a break for it, and ensconced Horseface in the kitchen and Fflageolet in the sitting room, where she told Lady Amanda to remain, on guard.

Flouncing off to the kitchen, her various necklaces and bracelets, mostly of shell, jangled as she strode into the domestic quarters, and sat down at the kitchen table to begin her interrogation of

71

how and what had actually happened, or was supposed to have happened.

Five minutes later, she was back. 'Horseface says she went into the bathroom last night and took her bracelet off, putting it on the washbasin while she had a quick shower. Having taken rather a lot of rum punch, she forgot it when she came out, and just went straight to bed. She said that when she went to retrieve it this morning, it was gone.'

'I swear to God I never even saw her rotten bracelet. I'd gone to the other bathroom to have a bit of a soak, and I only went into that one to use the "facilities" before I got into bed. I didn't see anything on the wash hand basin when I washed my hands after, um, you know,' protested the accused.

Windy was silent for a few moments, to consider her verdict. Finally, she said, 'Come on, we're all going up to that bathroom right now.' Calling Horseface from the kitchen, she put them into the order in which they had come downstairs, and led them straight to the wash hand basin in question.

Opening the cupboard beneath the basin, she extracted a wrench, and hauled at the bolt on the U-bend until it loosened. She then removed it by hand, and out fell a cascade of sparkling diamonds, strung together, with the addition of a few hairs and bits of toothpaste, on a white gold setting.

'There you go!' she said in triumph. 'These sinks have open plug-holes. This is not the first time something like this has happened, and it certainly won't be the last. May I suggest that you never leave anything precious on the surround of the basin, and always keep the plug in when the basin is not in use, so that nothing else can escape that way. Now, kiss and make up, like good girls.'

Horseface and Fflageolet glared at each other under beetling brows, still not quite certain that it had been a false alarm. 'Do as you are told! *Maintenant!*' – this had been her magic word as head girl – 'or I shall put you both in detention, and you shan't come out with us tonight!'

Slowly, the frowns and glares dissolved, and within a couple of minutes, both housemates were apologising to each other for what they had said and done during their rumble.

'Now, play nicely!' ordered Windy, and swept her way imperiously back outside. Lady Amanda followed, and when they were out of sight of villa number one, they both dissolved into laughter. 'It was just like old times, wasn't it?' chuckled Windy.

'And you haven't lost the power you had as head girl,' agreed Lady Amanda, with a big grin slapped across her face. 'You were absolutely marvellous. A dowager duchess couldn't have done better.'

'Oh, I say! Really, Sniffy?'

'Absolutely!'

'Get that Hugo of yours on to the starting blocks when you get back. Beep-Beep and I are going to have a bit of a round of pool games for the rest of the morning, then we're going to have a barbecue lunch in the shade of the palms. We can all have a siesta, or do a bit of house-viewing, this afternoon.

'This evening, I've got Winstone coming over again to take us, first to Uncle Obediah's Rum Keg Landing Beach Bar, actually on the beach, for a bit of a chill, then we'll go on to the Lizard Lounge for a bit of a bop. There are only cocktails there until about eight, then they start a disco. We can grab a bite whenever we want while we're there. There's always food on the go, for as and when customers want it. What do you think?'

'Ambitious programme, Windy, don't you think?' replied Lady A.

'Not if we all opt for the siesta, and do a viewing of the properties for sale en masse tomorrow. We'll all be as fresh as daisies after a couple of hours' snooze, post-luncheon. In fact, we'll all be raring to go again. Trust me. I've lived here for years.'

'Well, I might trust you, but I don't know if Hugo will.'

'I bet old Hugs will be really up for shaking his booty with all of us fine females,' replied Windy, with a confident smile.

'I shouldn't bet your shirt on it,' replied Lady Amanda, remembering the fiasco of their only visit to the ship's disco. 'It can get quite chilly here at night, or so I've heard, and he won't like that.'

But the planned viewing either this afternoon or the next day would have to be postponed.

Hugo was a bit grumpy upon being informed of the plans for the day, commenting that this was his first time in tropical parts; that it felt like his days were being as strictly timetabled as they had been at school, and that he wouldn't stand for it much longer. He finished this tirade with a heartfelt 'harumph', simultaneously expelling air through his nostrils, looking and sounding for all the world like a disgruntled walrus, and gave Lady Amanda a challenging look.

74

'Don't worry, Hugo. She'll get tired of it in a few days. She really just wants to sell us all some houses, so when she's done her bit as good-time party hostess and showcased the island, she'll get down to brass tacks, and we can all have a bit of a breather. Don't be an old stick-in-the-mud. You only live once,' she chided him.

'As long as this flatulent person doesn't cause me to die of exhaustion in the meantime. By the way, why was she called Windy at school?'

'If you think of what you've just said about her, you'll find you've hit the nail right on the head,' replied Lady A with a basilisk stare.

'Flatulence?' queried Hugo, his eyes almost popping out.

'Precisely. You should be safe enough today, though. She'll be eating barbecued food for lunch, and the amount of charcoal on that should help considerably. And, by the way, she referred to you as "Hugs" just now.'

Hugo's mouth fell open at this impertinence, and he scuttled upstairs as quickly as he could to get changed, hoping that he didn't find himself alone with this female windy wonder. His mother had been very sensible to carry a vinaigrette of smelling salts in her handbag – just in case. When they arrived at the back of Cocktails, both wearing T-shirts, Hugo in shorts, and Lady Amanda in a mid-calf cheesecloth skirt she had purchased in Belchester market, everyone else was in their costumes and in the water, happily playing with a variety of inflatables.

'Got your cozzies on under there?' called Wuffles, who was now sitting on the side of the pool getting her breath back. On receiving a reply in the affirmative, she continued 'Well, get on in here. We decided not to start the games until you two arrived. You're the last.'

'I don't know if I want to play games,' muttered Hugo into Lady A's ear.

'I think you'll find that you don't have much of a choice,' replied Lady Amanda, slipping off her outer clothes, and pulling her already-inflated pink ring round her middle. 'Last one in's a Brussels sprout!' And with this, she jumped into the pool, only to find it was so shallow that end that the ring didn't reach the water. 'Bother!' she exclaimed, and began to march doggedly out, sinking further and further as the water deepened.

Hugo sighed, and reluctantly removed his T-shirt and shorts, leaving his flip-flops until he got to the very edge of the pool and was just con-templating the water from halfway along it when a cry of 'Banzai!' distracted him, and Windy launched herself at him, having got out and crept up from behind. Both of them went into the water, Hugo screaming like a girl, with Windy clinging on determinedly round his waist.

When he finally resurfaced, puffing like a grampus, Windy had breast-stroked her way to the far end of the pool where the deepest water was, and waved at him impertinently, calling, 'Will you be my secret sweetheart, Hugs, dearest, if we can keep news of our romance from Beep-Beep?'

Hugo turned as red as a ... a ... very red thing, and doggy-paddled his way to the shallow end where he would be able to get his feet on the bottom. Forgetting what had just happened to his housemate, he misjudged where the metre mark might be, and ended up beaching himself, his ample stomach lifting him slightly out of the water, before he finally came to a standstill.

Before he could drown in embarrassment, if not in actual pool water, Windy shouted, 'Three cheers for Hugs. He's really got the tropical party spirit', and he had to hide his face as they all proceeded to do just that.

As the echoes of the cheers still rung under the garden palms, Enid and Beauchamp appeared. It would seem that they considered their marriage well and truly consummated now, and Windy had made sure she left a message on their answering machine, just in case they fancied venturing over to join in the compulsory fun.

Three cheers rang out again, for the newlyweds, and Enid went as crimson as Hugo had done just a minute or so ago. There were some rather obscene catcalls from the pool area, but these were ignored and their source remained unidentified. The old girls knew the ones who were the likely culprits, and treated their crude remarks with the contempt they deserved.

What happened next really caught Hugo and Lady A's attention. They had never seen Beauchamp in anything other than his impeccable butler's attire, or Enid in anything other than sensible, covering clothes. Now, they stripped down to their swimming attire, and Enid suddenly didn't look as old as she used to in her sensible tweeds and conservative frocks.

Granted, she had renewed a lot of her wardrobe with more colourful outfits since she had become engaged to Beauchamp, but Hugo and Lady Amanda still thought of her as an old dear. In her bikini she proved to be quite a bit younger and, watching from the poolside, Beep-Beep could appreciate why they had not emerged from their marital bed for so long.

Beauchamp's body was also a bit of a surprise as, although he was rather older than his new wife, he evidently kept in shape, making Lady Amanda suspect that somewhere, in the unused rooms of Belchester Towers, there must be quite a lot of gym equipment. Not only was he more hirsute than she would have guessed, but his musculature was well-developed, and he caused quite a few wolf-whistles of appreciation from the oldies there present.

They both jogged down to the deep end, held their noses in unison, and jumped simultaneously, not reappearing until they had swum underwater to the very middle of what was quite a large pool. The smattering of applause that greeted this act of synchronisation was quelled by a loud two-fingered whistle from Windy, who announced that the games were about to begin, and that she would organise them into teams for this.

As the smell of burning charcoal filled the air, they played in two teams, first passing a balloon through their legs and on to the next team member – Lady A electing to stand in the shallow end for this, others choosing the difficulty of the deep end, simply for the hilarity it caused as they tried to push an air-filled balloon down deep enough to pass between their knees.

Next, a net was seemingly effortlessly erected

across the pool, and a game of volleyball commenced, again, some of them electing not to be able to touch the bottom, others – wonder who? – choosing to stand in the shallowest water possible. It wasn't long, however, before the smell of barbecuing chicken and pork filled the air, and a halt was called before someone passed out with hunger. They had worked up quite an appetite with their games, and some of them were halfway out of the pool before Windy shouted, 'Let's debag Hugs again.'

The ensuing half-hour will remain undetailed, as Hugo fought fiercely to retain the security of what he considered to be his *very* private parts, his eventual defeat, and his language afterwards, as the old girls played with his swimming trunks, making quite a game of it before they let him put them back on before he got out of the water.

By this time, Enid and Beauchamp were the centre of attention, and it was only as the two old friends began to approach the area where Beep-Beep was handing round plates fragrant with barbecued corn, plantain, and meat, that Windy sidled up to them and asked if she could have a word with 'good old Sniffy' in private, later on.

Lady Amanda graciously agreed, although her mind immediately went into a foment of speculation, but she managed to contain it long enough to ask why Douglas, their darling Adonis, had failed to join them, yet again.

'I simply don't know what that boy gets up to when he's here. He comes out every four to six months, says he's got business to catch up with, and won't let anyone, not even a maid, into the house. He always takes the same villa, and asks me if I can save it till the last to sell. I suppose he wants to buy it at some point in the future, but he's really a mystery to me,' she explained, a nest of anxious wrinkles gathering in the centre of her forehead.

'He seems to be a law unto himself, but I can hardly refuse the rental. We could do with the cash. Anyway, least said, soonest mended, as we always used to say at dear old St Hilda's.'

With that, all three of them went towards the rest of the gang at the barbecue to collect their plates of food, Lady Amanda in a pensive mood, wondering what it was that Windy wanted to discuss with her that demanded absolute privacy: after all, she knew all the old girls. Why had she chosen her?

Rum punch was served with the food, although it proved to be a rather less potent mix than they had imbibed at the Parakeet Club the night before. Nevertheless, its soporific effects after their exercise in the sun and a bellyful of barbecued food meant that all the old girls opted for a siesta that afternoon to refresh themselves for the evening, and it was agreed that they would embark on the villa viewing the next day.

Catching Windy's eye just before they left, this most glamorous of the old girls approached them and said, 'I'll catch up with you later, Sniffy. I'll just give things a bit more thought before I pour out my heart to you.'

Whatever could she mean? Lady Amanda returned to their villa terribly frustrated at this delay in getting her teeth into what she considered would be a very juicy story, for Windy, after all, had been head girl, and Lady A just a humble ink monitor and prefect.

Chapter Seven

After a frustrating quarter of an hour, her mind swirling with thoughts about what Windy could possibly want to confide in her, Lady Amanda eventually slipped into the realm of the Sandman, waking only once, when Hugo shook her shoulder and said he could hear her snoring from the room across the landing; a fact she denied, but Hugo blamed on the alcohol she had drunk at lunch-time. She had snored occasionally on board ship, but Hugo had been so run ragged himself with the ghastly playfulness of the old ladies that he'd managed to ignore it and get back to sleep.

She awoke at five o'clock that afternoon, fresh as a daisy and ravenous: just time for a quick swoosh under the shower – mustn't forget her *bonnet de douche* – and to run a comb through her curly locks. Definitely time to approach Beauchamp about getting her roots seen to, she thought, as she reached for the hand mirror to check her rear view.

Hugo had also roused himself, and appeared on the landing wearing a pair of bright orange shorts and a T-shirt with Snow White and the seven dwarves on it, his hair fluffy from its recent meeting with that unusually exotic – for him – piece of equipment, the hairdryer.

81

As they were descending the stairs, they heard the hooting of the local bus, and the ringing of the doorbell. The others were evidently ready as well.

They were taken first to Old Uncle Obediah's Rum Keg Landing Beach Bar, or as close as they could get to it, for it was down on the sand, just above the water line. It was a small shack, roofed with dried palm fronds, its bar a piece of driftwood supported by lengths of bamboo, and behind it was a very small man, introduced to them as Short John Silver. The man's grizzled hair was greying and cut close to his scalp, his eyes a mid-brown, his smile toothy.

As he emerged from behind the bar, everyone new to the island noticed his slightly odd gait and, when he appeared, he laughed at their stares and explained that as a child, he had been involved in an argument with a truck, and lost his legs. After a couple of years crawling around on his stumps, he had been given prosthetics, and been lucky enough to have them ever since.

They were so short that Lady Amanda wondered if they'd ever been changed since that time. Certainly, he had a very long body, and his legs were definitely out of proportion to the size of his trunk, but he seemed happy enough to run his bar, and was already mixing them something he said was a Banana Daiquiri.

It took some time for them all to be given a long, cool glass, and by the time he had served the last of them, the first served were holding out their glasses for a refill. The drink was absolutely delicious, although it packed a punch (pardon the pun) that none of them realised at that moment.

With what seemed like unnecessary haste, Windy herded them back on to the old bus and they arrived a few minutes later at the Lizard Lounge. A few steps into the building, and they believed what their former head girl had meant about how it had got its name. Tiny lizards skittered across the floor, avoiding the hefty foot-steps of the new arrivals, and one or two of them screamed, and rushed outside again – the old girls, that was, not the lizards.

'Don't be silly girls; they won't hurt you,' called Windy after a couple of retreating backs. 'They're more frightened of you than you are of them.'

'I wouldn't put money on that,' replied Wuffles, who was actually trembling.

'Come back in and have a couple of cocktails. They're marvellous antidotes to irrational fears. A couple of Grasshoppers, and you'll be as right as rain.'

'I can't stand grasshoppers either,' wailed Wuffles, and Windy enquired,

'Of the alcoholic kind? Made with Crème de Menthe?'

'1 think I could tolerate a couple of those,' replied Wuffles, but still standing her ground just outside, until she was handed a glass containing a creamy emerald green liquid. Two glasses later, she had ventured inside to re-join the others.

'We're going to have a nice lobster salad here before the music starts, then we're going to boogie,' trilled Windy, smiling graciously at her charges, whom she considered should be very grateful she had such good island contacts to have arranged all the treats she had managed.

'I don't think I know how to boogie,' Hugo whispered in Lady A's ear.

'You don't have to do much,' she replied. 'You don't even have to move your feet – just sway and wiggle your botty a bit, then wave your arms around.'

'I don't think I could do all that without falling over,' he replied in a worried voice.

'Then do them in sequence: a few seconds of swaying, then a few seconds of botty action, then just wave your arms around for a bit, as if you're drowning. Would you be able to manage that?'

'Possibly, but I'll have to slip outside first and have a little practice.'

'Well, do it now, before we sit down to eat. I'll get you another cocktail.'

Hugo slipped out of a side door and commenced his first practice boogie. While he was gone. Lady Amanda approached Windy and hissed into her ear that she still had not had that private word she had requested.

'Not now, with everyone around. I'll catch you later, when everyone's gone to bed,' she replied, 'but you'll have to get rid of darling old Hugs too.'

Blast!

Droopy-Drawers, who had gone out of a rear door in search of the little girls' room, re-entered through a side door, and called out to Lady Amanda, 'I think you should come out here. Hugo seems to be having some sort of a fit. Is he prone to them?'

'Not as far as I know,' replied the erstwhile ink monitor, and followed her old friend outside.

One look explained everything. Hugo was trying to bop and boogie. Unexpectedly, Lady A suddenly broke into a lively body wiggle, stepping from side to side, and moving her arms rhythmically, and Hugo stopped, flabbergasted. 'I never knew you could do that!' he exclaimed.

'You never asked. Now, follow my movements as best you can, then we'll go inside and eat when you can manage to do "summat like".'

Hugo did as he was told, and Droopy-Drawers disappeared into the cocktail bar, disgusted that there had been no emergency after all.

The lobster dinner was fantastic, especially as it was accompanied by a fizzy white wine, even if this latter was of Californian origin. As soon as the plates were cleared away, Short John (who had closed down for a while, having no customers, and was helping out with the unexpected influx of customers here) began pushing the tables to the wall, and within a few minutes a steel band appeared at the far end of the space and the music had begun.

Hugo had a go at strutting his funky stuff, but when several people asked him if he was OK, and another asked if an insect was bothering him, he took a break and sat with Lady Amanda, who was saving her sassy moves for later on.

The place was filling up with locals now, but Lady Amanda, ever sharp-eyed and shamelessly nosy, noticed that one of their group kept disappearing out of the door to where she knew the 'facilities' to be located. Short John also kept taking small trips away from the bar, and she wondered if there had maybe been an instant attraction between the two. Horseface wasn't exactly easy on the eye, but there was no accounting for taste, and Short John wasn't exactly the most attractive of men either.

Halfway through the evening, Lady Amanda heard a small cheer go up near the entrance, and swivelled round to find that the Beauchamps had joined them, both of them in laid-back colourful clothes. Enid had on the ubiquitous kaftan that seemed to be the staple of female island clothing. Beauchamp was attired in a lilac T-shirt partnered with a batik sarong, and Hugo's eyes nearly fell out on to his lap. Beauchamp in a skirt? Whatever next? Had the world gone mad?

Neither he nor Lady Amanda knew what the two newcomers had been drinking, or whether they were just drunk on love and the tropical atmosphere, but they cleared the dance-floor, giving a display worthy of a couple years younger.

After her turn on the floor, Lady A made a last minute visit to the ladies' before they left, disturbing a whispered conversation between Horseface and Short John and apologised as she passed through where they had been standing, hoping she had not disturbed plans for a lovers' tryst.

Soon, it was time to go, but the band had other ideas, and urged them to form a conga line, while a fair number of them decided that this was the perfect time to light up a little 'smoke'. Playing as loudly as they could, they led the customers of the establishment out on to the beach, right along to Old Uncle Obediah's, round his bar, and back to the Lizard Lounge.

'What is that peculiar smell?' asked the old

prefect, sniffing the air in confirmation of her nickname of former days.

'It is rather pungent, isn't it?' agreed Hugo, his nose in the air, his nostrils twitching like those of a small mammal that scents danger.

'I believe you'll find that's marijuana, your ladyship,' Beauchamp's voice boomed in her ear.

'Shh! Someone might hear you and call the police,' from Lady A.

'What do you mean, "call the police"?' interjected Windy, who had been shamelessly eavesdropping. 'Most of the members of that band *are* the police, or what passes for the forces of law and order on this island.'

'Good grief!'

When Winstone had dropped them all off and they had dispersed to their various villas, Hugo gave an anguished squawk, and made a rush for the downstairs bathroom, from which, shortly, could be heard distressed moans and groans.

Knocking on the door, Lady Amanda enquired in a rather worried voice, 'Are you alright, Hugo?'

From within there came a hollow moan, and the reply, 'Not to put too fine a point on it, Manda, the world seems to be falling out of my bottom, and it burns like hell – excuse my language in the presence of a lady.'

'Have you been sick?' she called through the door.

'No, it's just that my bowels have turned to water, and it feels like I'm suffering from that delicacy I saw in the freezer centre when you took me round the shops in Belchester once –

Rings of Fire – only in my case, in the singular.'

'It must be something you've eaten. I'll give Windy a quick ring to see what she suggests. She hasn't had that private word with me yet, and I'm just dying of curiosity.'

There was another almighty groan, and she hurried to the telephone to seek advice as to the best treatment for her suffering housemate.

'Nothing to worry about, Sniffy. It'll be the island hot sauce from lunchtime. I forgot to warn you that it doesn't burn too much on the way down, but it feels like your bum's on fire when it decides to make its exit. I've got some soothing cream that I'll bring round. I also have an old-fashioned commode, if he thinks he might need it, otherwise he could be on the lavatory all night, or even find himself waking up and finding that it's too late. I'll get Beep-Beep to bring it over when I come with the cream,' Windy gabbled.

Oh Lord, and Maria had put the local hot sauce in their omelettes at breakfast time. It looked like Hugo's recent gastronomic past had finally caught up with him, although Lady Amanda felt perfectly OK. But then, she did have the digestive system of an old goat, as her late father used to say.

Getting back to the present, she said, 'But what about that private ch...' But the head girl had already hung up, so all that Lady Amanda could do was to relay the information she had been given through the firmly locked door of the downstairs bathroom, and wait at the door for the delivery of the soothing medicament.

Within a minute or two, she answered a peremptory knock at the door, and Beep-Beep was the first to enter, carrying a lightweight commode chair, his arms straight out in front of him, a disgusted look on his face, as if the thing had already been used. He headed up the stairs without a word, easily identifying Hugo's bedroom, in which he left his despised cargo.

He left again, still without speaking, while Windy called instructions for the use of the unguent she had delivered, and begged Hugo to open the door just a crack so that she could slip the container through. 'You'll feel much better after you've put a coat of this on the affected area,' she assured him.

Another hollow groan greeted the suggestion of actually touching the 'affected area', but they heard the lock slide back, and a hand crept through a crack just large enough for it to get through. 'Thank you.' The voice was feeble and pained, and Lady A and Windy exchanged a worried look.

'I say,' began Windy. 'Do you remember anyone from school who qualified as a doctor?' she asked, 'only we haven't got an ex-pat one here, and I thought it might be an added incentive to the sale of the villas if one of them contained a doctor. I could offer her rent-free accommodation if she were to come out of retirement just for the aches and pains of a few creaking old limbs.'

'What about Stinky Stenham?' queried Lady A, after a quick riffle through her memory bank.

'Grand idea. Well done, Sniffy,' replied Windy with a smile of triumph. 'Do you have any contact details for her?'

''Fraid not.'

'Never mind. I'll try Facebook, to see if I can track her down, if not I'll give some of the other girls a ring and see if any of them are still in contact with her.'

Both turned their heads as they heard the bathroom door open, and Hugo emerged looking drawn but with a tentative smile on his face. 'Ahhh!' he sighed. 'That's better. Thank you so much for the ointment,' he said, addressing his neighbour. 'Did someone try to poison me?'

'No. Just the revenge of the Caribbayan hot sauce at lunchtime. Beep-Beep's put a potty chair in your room in case you have any trouble in the night. It has been known to strike more than once,' she informed him, looking him up and down to check he really was alright.

'Windy, what was it you wanted to discuss with me in priv...' But, once again, her old friend cut her off, saying, 'I must get back to Beep-Beep. He does so like us to have a quiet little nightcap together before we go up to bed.'

'Well I never!' exclaimed a gob-smacked Lady A. 'First she has to talk to me about something urgently, then she avoids the subject every time I see her. Whatever is she up to? Either she wants to confide in me or she doesn't, and if she doesn't, why doesn't she just say so?'

'Pardon?' asked Hugo, who hadn't quite followed all that.

'You'd better get to bed and not hang around for explanations. We don't want you pooping your shorts in the hallway, do we?'

Hugo scuttled off, with as much urgency as he could manage in his gait.

Collapsing on to the huge sofa in the open-plan living room, a large gin and tonic in one hand, Lady Amanda suddenly wished that Beauchamp were here to make her a cocktail. How she missed their usual routine. Being on holiday was OK for a few days, but it didn't take long for it to pall, and for her to miss her usual pace of life and surroundings.

It was no good, she'd never sleep, so she finished her drink and decided to have a moonlit walk along the beach. It must have been the unaccustomed siesta that had robbed her of her usual bedtime eagerness to get some rest. And she had too much on her mind. Maybe the lazy swell and hiss of the waves on the sand would relax her enough for her to want to retire.

A short walk took her to the eastern side of Parrot Bay, where the moonlight sparkled on the tips of the wavelets, effortlessly dancing into oblivion on the shoreline. Just out to sea a little way, a dazzling white boat took her attention. What time was it? she thought, looking at her watch. Why, it was past one. Surely no one was going to moor at this time of night, or rather, the morning?

As her eyes became adjusted to the reduced light of outside, she noticed a very small boat bobbing over the waves towards it. Whoever could that be? Was it one of the residents of Parrot Bay? Why? What were they doing?

Squinting, she managed to see something passed from the white yacht to the smaller craft, but whatever it was, was too small for her to recognise. And she also noticed that there were no lights on the yacht. The only light came from the moon and stars. Surely a boat out at sea, especially this close to the shore, should be showing some lights even if it were just mast, port, and starboard?

Stepping back a little to the shelter of a highly scented bush, so that she didn't stand out as a silhouette on the shoreline, she watched the small craft come into shore, and be deflated, eventually being secreted in some dense shrubbery about fifty yards away. The figure then made for Parrot Bay again and, although far away, there was no mistaking that thatch of pure white hair and the gait. What was their erstwhile beloved up to now?

Taking her gaze from the figure, evidently on his way to his villa, her eyes caught the outline of someone else standing further up the beach. The dark shape of a tall man watching through a pair of binoculars – or at least that would explain why his arms were in the position they were. Within a few seconds, he had turned and begun to walk away, but he had a strange shambling way of walking that seemed to ring bells too. Whatever was going on, on this island? The only person she had met who walked a little like that was Short John Silver, and he was practically a midget.

Chapter Eight

After a very disturbed night, during which she was constantly being woken by Hugo rushing off to the bathroom with audible cries of 'Argh!' and 'Oh no, not again!', Lady Amanda awoke the next morning wondering if the things she had seen the night before from her hiding place on the beach had been real, or more a product of the exotic fumes she had inhaled while doing the conga. She'd have to tell Hugo and see what he thought. Then another thought struck her.

Good Lord, she had actually done the conga! How humiliating. Would she ever be able to live it down? On the other hand, all the others had joined in, so there was probably nothing to worry about, and none of the good folk of Belchester need ever hear about it.

Maria's alto tones filtered up to the first floor, informing the two house guests that she had breakfast prepared and laid out for them downstairs. 'Ah hee-ah Miz Winterbottom got a treat lined up for you all today,' she greeted them.

'I thought everyone was going to view the houses today,' countered Lady Amanda, as Hugo tucked into a huge plateful of fruit, his body obviously completely emptied out by his unfortunate experience with the local hot sauce.

'Oh, she decided dat you all hadn't seen all de beauties of de island yet. She going to take you to de market today, den lunch in de township, and on to a guided tour round some of de jungle,' the native maid explained with one of her white, toothy smiles.

'Good heavens!' exclaimed Hugo. 'This is getting to be more like work than a holiday. What about lazy days in the sun?'

'You'll have plenny of time for dat after she's finished convincing you dat dere's nowhere better on dis planet to live dan Caribbaya.'

'If we don't drop dead of exhaustion first.' Hugo again came up for air from his close attention to some melon slices to give this opinion.

'She just love dis place and want everybody else to love it too.'

'And to sell her dratted houses,' added Lady A. 'No, no omelette for me today, Maria. I got away with it yesterday but I'm unlikely to be that lucky twice.'

At this, Hugo nodded his head vigorously, and Maria gave him a Paddington stare. 'So it was you dat had de trouble in de downstairs bathroom yesterday,' she stated pointedly.

'I'm so sorry. I meant to be up early so that I could do something about it myself,' Hugo apologised, swallowing a mouthful of mango.

'Never you worry, Mr Hugs. Dat's my job, and visitors don't usually make de same mistake twice,' she informed him.

'What did you call me?' Hugo asked in indignation.

'Why, what Miz Winterbottom tole me to call you: Mr Hugs.'

'If you wouldn't mind, I'd prefer it if you simply called me Hugo. It is my given name, after all.'

'No worries.' Maria was cool with that.

There was no time for Lady Amanda to talk to Hugo about *her* worries after breakfast, as there was the tootling of a horn outside, and once more the battered old bus, Winstone Churchill at the wheel again, waited for them outside for today's 'adventure in paradise'.

Many of the old girls were already assembled and climbing aboard as the occupants of number

94

fifteen left the house, noticing that, once more, there was no sign of Douglas Huddlestone-Black. One would hardly know he was on the island, thought Lady Amanda as she, for the second day in a row, nicked the window seat. Maybe she should ask about him again. She knew he was there because she had seen him the night before. Probably.

'Hey, Windy, where's our Adonis? Is he not joining us for anything? This is a huge reunion, after all,' she called to the front of the vehicle where Windy Winterbottom was sitting.

'Actually, he's scheduled to go home today,' she called back.

'What? But we've only been here five minutes,' shouted back Lady Amanda in surprise. The engine of the old crate really was noisy.

'That's what he's like. Sometimes he's here for three or four weeks, others, it's only a couple of days. The only way I usually know he's gone is that I find the villa keys in my mail box.

'So much for a holiday romance,' was shouted from the back of the bus, followed by some giggling.

'But we've still got dear old Hugs,' came next, and that set everyone off except, of course, for Hugo and Lady Amanda, who thought this all rather childish. Just because they had all been at school together didn't mean they could act like the children they had once been. Even if sometimes it seeped, unsought, to the surface.

It wasn't far to the market, but then nothing was far away on this small piece of land spewed out from the sea by a volcano, millennia ago.

Evidence of this creation still existed in the mountain to the north-west.

They heard the market before they saw it. Steel bands competed from different sides; traders shouted the superiority of their wares, children whooped and laughed as they ran and played, and the conversation of the women was, by necessity, at a high volume for them to be heard above the general cacophony.

As well as assaulting the ears, the market was also a visual treat, being inhabited by myriad colours and patterns, wandering around as they were worn, or held up for sale. Every woman, it seemed, had on a blindingly bright kaftan and a matching head wrap, and these items were the main ones on sale, apart from fresh produce and locally made jewellery, a fair sample of which had turned up on Windy's person since the beginning of their stay.

Above all the other noise a high-pitched tinkling and jingling came from dangling earrings, bracelets for both wrist and ankle, and necklaces. This descant was joined by the clonking and chatter of wind chimes made out of both bamboo and shells, and added something unforgettable to the scene that they were all about to enter and try to merge into.

After a couple of souvenir purchases, Lady A dragged Hugo off to a stand with some rough benches that sold coconut water and ordered two. The coconuts were served with just their tops cut off, and a straw added, and were very refreshing. In this haven in the maelstrom of commercial activity going on around them, Lady Amanda confided what she believed she had seen last night.

'I don't think you get hallucinations with weed,' Hugo assured her, wondering where on earth he had picked up this interesting factoid.

'Then it must be true. We must go looking for that boat he stashed when we can get away from "unsere Fuhrerin",' she decided. 'It all looks very fishy to me. First we see him sneaking out of a high-class shop in the jewellery quarter when he wasn't supposed to be going there. He doesn't show at any of the social stuff, not even bothering to have a chat with us.

'The only words he spoke to us were when I heard those very suspicious noises on the cruise ship on our way over here, and now Windy says he's leaving today. Maybe we should try to get hold of the keys so that we can have a good nose round where he's been staying. That man is definitely up to no good.'

'If you'd only curb your impatience, we're going to be taken round the houses tomorrow. Your old mate just wants to get on with making us fall in love with the place before she gives us the hard sell,' replied Hugo, appearing much more worldly-wise than usual. It must be the heat, thought Lady Amanda. It had woken some of his dozing brain cells, like some sort of latter-day Frankenstein's monster. If he started wearing a bolt through his neck she'd have to have a word with him.

'You're perfectly right, old stick,' she agreed, without missing a beat. 'And I'll probably be able to get Windy on her own tomorrow, for whatever it is she wants to tell me, but never actually gets round to. Come on, let's have another little toddle and see if there's anything else we can't live without buying before we have to get back on the bus.'

'Where are we lunching?' asked Hugo.

'You do nothing but think of your stomach.' commented Lady Amanda. 'You've hardly finished breakfast and you're already on to the next meal mentally. Actually, we're going into the township for lunch, so there should be lots of local dishes to sample. I hope so anyway.'

Hugo wasn't as enthusiastic about local recipes, after his run-in with the Caribbayan hot sauce, and determined to check that it wasn't in any of the dishes that he consumed. Last night and during it was an experience he never wanted to repeat as long as he lived, and he blushed with belated shame again at the state in which he had had to leave a certain piece of sanitary ware in the bathroom for Maria to find this morning.

For the rest of their visit to the market, Lady A's mind continued to mull over all the inexplicable or curious things that had happened since they had arrived. Had Horseface really been flirting with Short John, and had they set up a date? What had Adonis been doing out in that dinghy in the early hours, and who was the mysterious man watching his clandestine little sea trip?

These and many other things raced round and round in her head until it was time to get into that old bucket of a bus again, to drive into the nearby township where Windy had told them they would pick up a local guide for their trip into the jungle.

Lunch was an extravaganza of local produce and dishes, set out in the shade of a group of palms just off the township's square, and provided delicious, if suspiciously spicy dishes, but Hugo was very careful what he ate. The meats, however, were melt-in-the-mouth tender, and the fish, although a little on the hot side, deliciously flavoured. The plantains were, as usual, moreish and filling, and all members of the group hoped they weren't expected to walk through the forest, as they'd all rather made beasts of themselves. Again.

Winstone loaded a bus full of rather soporific passengers back into his care, and drove the few miles to the outskirts of the jungle area of the island where, fortunately, a couple of open-backed jeeps fitted with seats were ready to take them on their exploration into the mysteries of the wildlife, resident in the thick tropical growth. The island was certainly well-provided for with ways and means of getting that extra buck out of the day tourists, and evidently drives through a bit of the jungle were on the list.

The two local drivers looked like twins, with their gold-toothed smiles and corn-rowed hair, and politely helped the old biddies up and into their seats for the trip. On the transfer from vehicle to vehicle, there had already been a few squawks of alarm at the insects, both in the air and on the ground, and it didn't bode well for the rest of the afternoon.

Although there were audible signs of life under the great canopy of trees, there were no visible signs of it, with the exception of a flock of brightly coloured birds that flew overhead, just below the level of the treetops, and there were many squeals and moans about those who had phobias about snakes and spiders. In fact, Wuffles seemed to have a phobia about all insect life, and spent the whole time she was jostled round in the back of the jeep bundled up into a ball of pure fear, her eyes tight shut, her fingers in her ears.

The whole trip turned into such an unnerving experience that it was cut short, and they returned to the comparative safety of the bus in half the time they were supposed to be off it. The market may have been a colourful local experience, but the jungle was just too hardcore for most of the women. It was too alien an environment for them to either feel comfortable in or appreciate.

Windy decided instead that they would grab their beachwear and get Winstone to take them to the lagoon, and she would instruct her house staff to make ready a picnic which could be driven down to them later. There were permanent barbecues built at the lagoon, and picnic tables and benches, so they needed nothing else except for provisions.

The suggestion was accepted with sighs of relief, and when they got back to Parrot Bay, the old chums scuttled off with unexpected agility to collect what they needed. Windy followed Lady Amanda into her villa, and finally 'fessed up about what she wanted to consult her about.

While Hugo was upstairs looking out what he needed, the ex-head girl pulled an envelope out of her handbag and just handed it to her old school chum, her face a blank. Lady A took out the single sheet of paper and unfolded it, to find a message made out of letters cut from what looked like a number of different publications. 'I know what you are up to. I will be in touch,' was all it said.

'When did this come?' asked Lady Amanda, turning it over to ascertain there was nothing on the other side of the paper.

'The evening you all arrived here,' replied Windy.

'By post? What was the postmark?'

'By hand.'

'I see, so you think that one of us is responsible for it?'

'I can't see any other explanation, can you? The cut-out letters definitely don't come from the island's weekly newspaper; they seem to be from a variety of sources. How could it be a local?'

'And what exactly are you up to?' Lady Amanda was nothing, if not blunt.

'Nothing for you to worry about,' replied Windy, her eyes dropping and moving from side to side in a very guilty way.

'Are you sure you wouldn't like to tell me?' Lady Amanda's curiosity was fully roused, and she scented a mystery coming on.

'Oh, it's nothing important,' came the reply, and Windy once again scanned the floor on either side of her feet. 'Nothing for you to worry about.'

'Do you suspect anyone?' It was time to get to the nub of the matter.

'I did wonder if it was Fflageolet. Maybe in the intervening years since she used to help herself to our personal possessions, she might have pro-gressed into more adult ways of making unearned money, blackmail being one of them.'

'But it was proved that she never took that tennis bracelet. You found it yourself in the sink's

U-bend. It is possible that she's grown out of the habit and this is from someone else entirely,' countered Lady A.

'I know. It's just a feeling I've got. Hugo was talking about some adventures you've had together, solving crimes or something – I wasn't really listening – and I wondered if you'd have a snoop round here, to see if you can unearth anything incriminating.' Windy's face wore a pleading expression and, as her request had appealed to her old friend's rather large ego, Lady Amanda immediately accepted the commission, resolving to confide in Hugo as soon as she could, to see what he thought.

As an after-thought, she asked if Windy had talked to the local police about it. 'Well, that's just the thing: we don't have a police force as such. Although I referred to some of the band members the other night as "police", what we actually have is an island security force, provided by the owner of most of the island. If anything serious happens, they have to bring real police in from the mainland.'

'Oh,' said Lady Amanda, an unusually short answer for her.

As the bus disgorged them on to the shore of the lagoon, the sound of a retreating motorboat could be heard, disappearing up the coastline. Boats didn't normally enter the lagoon, but there was some evidence that this one had, as its wake was still very slightly visible where the waters flowed through the narrow channel to the sea. Windy suggested that it might have been someone after a bit of fishing, and dismissed the subject, while the rest of the party stripped down to their swimming costumes.

Lady Amanda set her towel down in the shade of a palm, and motioned Hugo to join her. This was the earliest opportunity for her to confide in him, and she fancied a bit of a gossip. Everything was always such a whirlwind with Windy that Lady A suddenly remembered that it wasn't just her flatulence that had spawned her school nickname.

She had just opened her mouth to start telling her tale of blackmail, when there was some furtive movement amongst the large ferns about ten yards away. Holding her right forefinger to her lips and nudging Hugo, she pointed, and they watched as a tall figure rose and made off slowly into the undergrowth, his progress soon masked by the gloom of the shady trees.

'Now who, I wonder, was that?' she asked in a hushed voice, lest the sound should carry. 'He seemed somehow familiar, and yet unfamiliar at the same time.' For a flash, she remembered again the watching figure she saw from her hiding place in the scented bush on the edge of the beach.

'I know what you mean,' replied Hugo, looking puzzled. 'I thought at first it was someone we'd met, then it seemed that it wasn't. I wonder why we both feel like that?'

'So do I,' replied Lady A, setting her mind to unravel this rather unusual event.

'Do you think the boat was dropping off a local?' asked Hugo, who thought he might have the answer.

'You'd think so, but why, then, was he hunkered

down in the ferns? Why didn't he just walk away from the lagoon?'

'Call of nature?' suggested Hugo.

'He would've been standing up ... ooh, *that* sort of call of nature. I'm going over there to have a look,' decided the intrepid Lady A.

'Manda, that's absolutely disgusting.' Hugo wrinkled his nose in distaste.

'No, it's not. It's what any detective worth his or her salt would do. I won't be a minute.' She was back very quickly. 'Nothing whatsoever there, not even a whiff,' she informed her companion, as he looked at her with disapproval.

'How could you!' he exclaimed.

'Well, at least we know that whatever he was doing, he wanted to do it in private,' she replied stubbornly. He was up to no good, you mark my words. I just wish I could place who he reminded me of.'

Hugo stayed out of the water because he didn't fancy losing his trunks again and pleaded, as an excuse, that the movement of the waves made him feel dizzy. Lady Amanda stayed dry too, as she explained that she had a hole in her ring. At this, there was an explosion of laughter from Hugo, and she looked at him in disapproval.

'In my rubber ring, you fool. Really, old stick, you have a mind like a sewer at the moment. You're getting as bad as that lot in the water.'

'Sorry, Manda. I think the heat must be affecting my mind.'

'I wasn't aware you took it out of the house with you, in case you lost it,' our intrepid investigator replied, and crossed her arms in triumph, as she trumped his ace.

At number five Parrot Bay, Douglas Huddle-stone-Black had just struggled downstairs with the last of his suitcases, about to ring for the local taxi to pick him up for his ferry to the next island where he would be able to catch his plane back to good old Blighty, when there was a soft knock on the back door of his villa.

The top of it was obscure glass, so he could not define exactly who his visitor was, but it was certainly a tall person. With a sigh of exasperation at this interruption, he walked towards it and flung it open, looking up in surprise at the figure standing there. 'Whatever's going on?' he asked in puzzlement, before a fist knocked him to the ground.

Back in the villa that evening, the two of them were having a quiet time, with just the nearest they could find to a ploughman's lunch for their supper which included goat's cheese instead of good, old, reliable Cheddar – when there was a banshee wail from outside, which got louder as it approached their property, followed by a thunderous knocking on the door.

At the sound of a damsel in distress, it was Hugo who got to the door first, and Lady Amanda had a small smile of smugness at how successful the operations to replace his damaged joints had been, although they would never be perfect again. He was so much more mobile than when she had first found him, languishing in a third-rate nursing home, with nothing to look forward to other than his own death.

It was in rescuing him that they had come across their first taste of solving crimes, and had been avid amateur sleuths ever since, Lady Amanda always on the hunt for something that needed her very special talent of sticky-beaking. And if all the little unexplained things that had happened since they embarked upon this holiday came to something, she reckoned this could be their fifth mystery, just waiting to be solved.

Hugo pulled open the door to admit a siren of a figure – but an emergency siren rather than a beautiful one who lured sailors on to rocks with her hypnotic and enchanting song. Windy's mouth was so wide open that one could see her epiglottis. Approaching this embodiment of distress, Lady Amanda gave her a sharp slap round the chops, then stood back as the yelling subsided into muffled sobs, coupled with a few rich swear words, as criticism of her precipitate cure for hysteria.

'That's better,' she soothed their shocked visitor. 'I'll just get you a brandy while Hugo gets you seated, then you can tell us all about what's got you into this state.' Windy subsided on to a feather-stuffed sofa and slumped there, hiccoughing in distress.

After she had had a few gulps at the enormous brandy with which she was presented, she looked at Hugo and Lady Amanda, and said baldly and in a sepulchral voice, 'He's dead!'

'Who's dead?' squeaked Lady A. 'Not Beep-Beep? Surely not. He looked as fit as a flea only this afternoon.'

106

Windy's head began to shake to and fro, and eventually she managed, 'It's Adonis.'

'Douglas Huddlestone-Black? But I thought he was leaving today. That's what you told me earlier.'

'So I did, but when his keys weren't in our mailbox when I was getting ready for bed, I thought I'd just pop over and see if everything was alright. I have a spare, as he only rents it, and it might need some repair or maintenance work when he's not here.

'I let myself in, and his cases were in the hall, but they were open, and everything was pulled out of them and his stuff strewn all over the floor and the bottom of the staircase.'

'Weren't you scared?' asked Hugo.

'Not in the least, although I expect I ought to have been. But, being good old Windy, I just thought he'd mislaid his passport and was probably upstairs pulling apart the drawers in the bedroom to see if he'd left it up there. And up the stairs I toddled calling out "Coo-ee", like the fool I was acting.'

'Why were you a fool?' Hugo was definitely interested in getting to the end of this story, because he sensed a juicy conclusion to it.

'And there he was. On the bedroom floor. His throat cut from ear to ear. Dead. And the killer could have still been in the villa, for all I knew. What an idiot I was to go charging up there calling out.'

'And you heard and saw no one?' Lady Amanda was on the case now. 'Have you called anybody?'

'There's nobody to call on the island. I told you so. We have to get police from the mainland.'

'And how do you get in touch with them?'

'By satellite phone.' Windy was a little calmer now.

'Then get Beep-Beep to make the call, tell the authorities that there's been a murder, then take us over there so that we can have a little snoop around first, in case the police miss something.'

'Do you really think we ought to, Manda?' Hugo was always much more law-abiding than Lady A, who could be a law unto herself.

'Of course we must. When you think about it, there can't be that many suspects. How many people did he know on the island apart from ourselves? It is our duty to find whatever evidence there is, so that there's not a miscarriage of justice.'

'She's right, you know,' agreed Windy, who had quickly popped back home to instruct Beep-Beep to get on the blower, then returned to lead them to the scene of the crime. 'I've brought some washing-up gloves with me so that we don't leave any fingerprints,' she declared, handing over two pairs to her co-conspirators, and they noticed that she had hers on already.

'No wonder you made head girl,' was Lady A's only comment, before they went over to number five Parrot Bay to view the murdered body of the boy with whom they had all been in love in their school days.

'Of course, they'll have to take his body to the mainland for a post mortem,' whispered Windy as they walked the short distance to the House of Death. 'We simply don't have the facilities here.'

'That's going to string things out a bit, isn't it?' Lady Amanda was also whispering, although whether it was so as not to alert a gaggle of fussing old women, or because of the gravity of the situation and the darkness, she didn't know. The sun set early here, all year round, and darkness did tend to make people act a little furtively.

'I just hope it's not one of us,' replied Windy, not really confirming or denying Lady A's worries about timescale.

'Who else did he know?' she asked. 'Did he ever go out for a drink or a meal?'

'Occasionally, but not often.'

'Well, that helps to widen the field of suspects,' concluded Hugo, optimistically.

They entered the villa in total silence, the two who hadn't already been there looking round in shock at the mess of belongings just hurled hither and thither as someone had emptied the waiting suitcases. 'It looks to me more like someone looking for something they thought he had. I'm quite sure he was far too organised to mislay a thing as important as his passport,' said Lady Amanda.

'I tend to agree with you,' commented Windy, taking a couple of deep breaths before they mounted the stairs. On the landing, she stopped and pointed to an open door. 'If you don't mind, I'd rather not see what's in there again. I'll wait here.'

Lady Amanda went first, wondering at the way Hugo could now climb stairs without the agony and effort it had once cost him. Once inside, her whole mind was riveted on the gory scene that lay before them. Douglas Huddlestone-Black lay on the white bedside rug, the biggest smile ever plastered right across his neck and gleaming redly at the newly arrived visitors.

Just outside the doorway, there was a fanfare on the bum-trumpet. Any stress went straight to Windy's digestive system.

'Speak on, sweet lips that never told a lie,' intoned Lady Amanda, while Hugo covered his nose with his hand to ward off the noxious fumes which were already pervading the room.

Chapter Nine

The police arrived at six o'clock the next morning – what Lady Amanda referred to as sparrow-fart, in her bleary-eyed state as the noise of the helicopter's rotors woke her. They had no sooner stopped when there was the roar of a powerful engine, and a police boat pulled in as far as it could to Parrot Bay, disgorging officers with their shoes in one hand, their trousers rolled up to their knees.

That was followed by the noisy chatter of other officers arriving from the clearing south-west of the lagoon, where the helicopter had landed, and the whole crew descended on number five. There were a number of police officers, a photographer/videographer, and a fingerprints man included. The medical man had come in the helicopter, by which means it was intended the body should be taken away for the autopsy.

By the time they had been in the house fifteen minutes, there was a cackling gaggle of oldies outside the front door, all craning their necks and squinting to see what was going on inside. Beep-Beep did not join them, but Windy, Lady Amanda and Hugo were the last to arrive, knowing full well what was beyond everyone's view inside, and having taken the time to steel themselves against the barrage of questions they would inevitably face, not only from the police, but from the other temporary and permanent residents of Parrot Bay.

Some of the girls had taken time to throw on some clothes, others were still in their nighties, with a dressing gown carelessly thrown over the top for decency's sake, and they were all suffering a severe case of bed-head.

'What the blithering heck's going on here?'

'What's happened and when did it occur?'

'Who's dead? Anyone?'

'Why are there police here?'

'Where's Adonis? Is he hurt?'

The questions were many, but all on the same theme. Something momentous had occurred, and no one had told them about it. With a telepathic precision, the three who knew very well what was going on advised everyone to wait until the police informed them of what the trouble was and the trio kept schtum. There was a tacit understanding between the three of them that life would be a little easier that way. Their questioning would be less rigorous if the others had the initial facts from the police horse's mouth, so to speak.

Having pleaded ignorance by a sin of omission, Lady Amanda looked around at the other old girls' faces to see what emotion was being shown in light of this unexpected arrival of officialdom. Was it a shock to all of them, that something had summoned the police from the mainland? Or did someone know what lay in the master bedroom of that innocent-looking villa, with a gaping slash across its throat?

Most of the faces were worried and puzzled, but a few of them showed a different emotion. Eeyore, for some reason, looked absolutely furious but devastated at the same time, although Lady A could think of no reason why she should be. Horseface looked as guilty as hell about something, and Longshanks looked worried to death. Whatever was eating these three? Could one of them possibly be responsible for this vile and bloody death? Surely not!

One of the policemen, dressed in a short-sleeved shirt and knee-length uniform shorts came outside and, holding up his hands, palms outwards, for silence, began to address the small crowd of twittering oldies that had gathered outside.

'Attention, please. This house is now out of bounds, as it is a crime scene. There has been a suspicious death here, and we shall need to speak to you all individually, once we are satisfied that we are finished examining the property for now. I should like you to wait in your houses until one of my officers comes round to interview you about the deceased.'

Dammit, he'd used the words 'suspicious death' and 'deceased'. Now they knew there was probably murder afoot! DI Pharaoh was mortified at what he had just let slip, and disappeared into the villa again with a burning face. It was due to the gathering of elderly ladies that he had been wrong-footed: they made him think of his grandmother, and he could never lie to her.

The girls dispersed, talking in pairs and trios about the now indisputable fact that there was a murderer at large, and it was highly likely that Adonis had been the victim. Lady Amanda stumped back to number fifteen, Hugo trotting behind trying to keep up with her. This warm weather really was doing their mobility the world of good.

When they got back to the villa, Hugo asked her what she thought about what would happen now that the police had arrived. 'Shh!' she chided him. 'I've got a lot of thinking of do,' and she disappeared off into the large airy living room and headed straight to the drinks cabinet. Pouring herself a sherry, which she tossed off in one, she made to leave the house.

'Where on earth are you going?' asked Hugo, now thoroughly puzzled by her actions.

'I'm going to visit all the others. Windy asked me yesterday to find out who had sent her an anonymous letter, and that's exactly what I intend to do. If I can pick up the scent of a murderer as well as a blackmailer on my travels, well, all the better,' she explained.

'Can't I come too?' asked her housemate, with a pout. He didn't want to be left out of any sleuthing that she might want to do.

'Best not. There ought to be someone in when the police call. You could go round to Windy's and see what she's got to say about what we should tell them.'

'Pardon?'

'Whether she wants to tell them that we saw

what was in there, too.'

'Gotcha!' Hugo was getting quite up on out-of-date slang, now he lived with other people. He had been alone too long, and relished the company this new lease of life had given him, since his rescue from that dreadful Birdlings Serenade Rest Home, and the bedridden existence he had eked out there.

Thus emboldened by sherry, Lady Amanda started by calling at West Indies Retreat where Eeyore, one of the permanent residents, lived, deciding on the short walk, that she would have to blast Enid and Beauchamp out of bed and into the investigation. Their behaviour simply wasn't good enough, considering the serious turn of events that had just occurred.

Eeyore opened the door, her eyes red and full of tears. 'Come in,' she sniffed. 'Sorry about this, but I still had the most dreadful crush on him, which I didn't realise until I saw him get off the boat again. It happens every time he comes over, just when I think I've got over it for the umpteenth time.' She stopped for a moment to blow her nose, standing aside so that Lady Amanda could enter. 'I had no idea I still felt that way yet again, and to find that he was dead was devastating.'

At this, she burst into a fresh cascade of tears, and Lady A put her arm around her and escorted her into the sitting room. 'You never married, did you?' she asked gently.

Eeyore's normally lugubrious face looked even more tragic, as she shook her head. 'I suppose that subconsciously, I always carried a torch for him,' she said quietly. They sat in silence for a moment, then Lady Amanda asked, 'You're a year-round resident here. When did you last see Adonis – Douglas, I should say?'

'Not since he arrived here and got off the boat. I was waiting at the quay and just got a glimpse of him as he hared off,' was the reply.

'Do you know why he seemed to lead such a secretive life when he was here, because Windy's told me he rarely socialised.'

'I have no idea. When he first started coming out here, I used to go round with cakes that I'd baked, but he wouldn't even answer the door to me, and I used to end up leaving them on the doorstep. I never wondered what he did with his time. I just wanted to spend some of it with him.'

What a pathetic case poor Eeyore was, thought Lady A, but could this be a cake too far for the spurned victim of unrequited love? Changing the subject so that she could chew over this idea in peace later, she asked her if she knew of anyone who might have a grudge against Windy and Beep-Beep, or who might know something to their detriment.

Eeyore seemed to be shocked by the idea that anyone could wish this couple ill-will. 'Why, they're the life and soul of Parrot Bay,' she said, 'if not the whole island.' Then she muttered, 'Oh, my poor, darling, beautiful Adonis,' and burst into a fresh cataract of tears. Lady Amanda took her leave to allow the woman to grieve in peace.

She had only walked back as far as her own villa when the sherry suddenly wore off, and she questioned her intention of going round the whole of the little community and poking her nose into other people's business. There must be a more subtle way than this, she thought, as she wandered back indoors and stood in the hall in a reverie of indecisiveness.

Suddenly she realised why Eeyore had looked both furious and devastated when she heard about what had happened to Douglas Huddlestone-Black. He was finally beyond her reach for the rest of her life, and there was no hope left of ever getting him to fall for her. Not only that, but she'd never again get the chance of even just catching a glimpse of him as he disembarked at the cruise terminal. She'd never have another chance to seduce him with her baking.

It would never have happened, of course, but all the time he had been alive, she could live with the hope that one day he would fall for her irresistible charms – or cakes; whichever he found the more attractive.

Before Hugo could get out of the sitting room, there was a knock on the door which, incidentally, Hugo answered, as Lady Amanda seemed too lost in deep thought to react to anything as prosaic as a doorknocker being used, and he opened it to find Beauchamp and Enid standing there, hand in hand.

'Good day to you, Mr and Mrs Beauchamp,' Hugo greeted them with a smile. 'How very good to see you two up and about.' Having thought about the implications of his last remark, he turned a light shade of pink, and ushered them into the house. 'Manda, we've got visitors. It's Beauchamp and Enid, come to see us.'

'Finally got yourselves out of bed, have you?' she said gruffly, conveniently forgetting that they had attended a couple of other group events such as the boogying at the Lizard Lounge, as she rejoined the land of the living. ''Bout time, though.'

'Manda, don't make such personal remarks,' Hugo chided her.

''Snot personal, it's just the truth,' she stated, ever forgetful. 'I suppose you've heard what's happened?'

'That's why we're here,' replied Beauchamp, as Enid covered her blushes as best as she could at Lady A's rather near-the-knuckle and inaccurate remarks.

'I was just on my way round to speak to everyone, but I only got as far as the house across the road. Eeyore's in bits, because she obviously had a bit of a thing about our Adonis since we were at school, but when I came out, I thought it would look a bit ham-fisted if I just called on everyone. I'd have completely blown my cover if I'd wanted to investigate. There's got to be a more subtle way of getting everyone to talk, but not to appear to be being too nosy.'

'Of course there is, and we came straight round as soon as I thought of it,' replied Beauchamp, looking just a mite smug.

'Come on then, spit it out, and don't leave us both in suspenders,' Lady A chivvied him.

'If I can use a laptop, I could print out invitations to a cocktail party here tonight. You can invite everyone round. Enid wouldn't mind doing canapés' – at this Enid nodded in agreement – 'and I can be responsible for cocktails. You've told

117

everyone how well I make them, but I've never actually mixed any for them. I'm sure they'll be glad to get together to talk about what's happened, as well as having some of my famous recipes: free food and booze. It's an irresistible combination, especially when you add in a pinch of local gossip and murder most foul.'

'And you really wouldn't mind doing the canapés, Enid?'

'Not at all. It would be good to feel useful again – domestically speaking – and it would be nice to have some varied company – nothing personal, you realise?' She directed this last to her husband, but he took it in good part, and merely smiled down at her.

'We could put a note on the invitations for everyone to bring a little something along, just to help the food go a bit further. The more food there is, the longer they'll stay, and the longer they stay, the more they'll drink. And, of course, the more they drink, the looser their tongues will become,' Beauchamp finished on a triumphant note.

'You are a genius, Beauchamp; and Enid, you're a brick, as always. Thank you both so much. You're absolutely right; alcohol loosens tongues and removes inhibitions. We'll be alright as long as Hugo doesn't do his naked clog dance on the terrace,' said Lady A with a twinkle in her eye.

'My what?' asked Hugo, scandalised.

'It was only a joke, Hugo. You didn't think I was serious, did you?'

'I just hoped you weren't. Do you think we'll be able to go next door and use their equipment for these invitations,' he replied.

'Another genius in our midst. Enid, you can word the invitations, and Beauchamp can have a look round Windy and Beep-Beep's extensive stock of booze to see if there's anything you might need for the cocktails. She won't mind at all. I've had a look in her larder, which isn't a larder at all: it's like a drinks warehouse. She must ship it here by the container-load. Come on, you lot. We've got a cocktail party to organise.'

Lady Amanda was so excited at what they had planned, involving four sets of ears instead of just one, and having everyone in the same villa, that she almost asked her co-conspirators if they wanted to do the conga round to their host and hostess's house. It must have been the last fumes of the sherry wafting away.

Windy and Beep-Beep were enchanted with the idea of a cocktail party for everyone next door, and Beep-Beep led Beauchamp to their booze cupboard – almost like a small room – while Windy got two shopping trolleys from her large understairs cupboard, in which to transport back the array of bottles that Beauchamp would no doubt need.

'Tell him not to be sparing with how many bottles he takes. We won't empty them all, and it's so much cheaper over here or from the mainland. I've heard so much about his expertise in mixing cocktails that I can't wait to taste some, and I don't want him to stint on ingredients,' she said.

Hugo went off to relay this information to the other two men and deliver the shopping trolleys, and also became entranced by the number and variety of the bottles in the store. He kept pointing at various shelves and exclaiming with delight at each new find. 'This is even better than Manda's drinks assortment, and I thought she had just about everything in it,' he said, with glee.

'It is rather marvellous, isn't it?' replied Beauchamp, with more enthusiasm in his voice than Hugo had ever heard before, except in his wedding vows. The man seemed to be absolutely bowled over, and in cocktail-mixing heaven.

As the butler loaded bottles into the two-wheeled conveyances, Beep-Beep said, 'You can always come back for more if you need them. It takes a great deal of ingredients to get cocktails just right, in my humble opinion.'

'I couldn't agree with you more,' beamed Beauchamp, his eyes twinkling at the prospect of getting his hands on some of these exotic concoctions. He had, of course, brought his own shaker with him. He never went anywhere without it; it was his form of a badge of office.

Back in the sitting room, Lady Amanda asked Windy if she had had any more 'communications'. 'Not so far,' she replied, 'but no doubt this murder has thrown the blackmailer off kilter, and we'll have to wait until he or she gets over the shock. I mean it must be one of us, mustn't it?'

'I would have thought the anonymous letter' – Lady Amanda sank her tones to a whisper for these last two words – 'must be from one of the old girls, but I can't be sure about the murder. Do you really think one of us could be so angry or so lost in love with the man that they would murder him?'

'I haven't the faintest idea at the moment. It all

seems too ghastly to be true,' replied Windy, her face a picture of confusion. 'This party tonight should give you a chance to really have a dig into what's going round the grapevine, though. Hugo told me you two had sorted out murder cases before.'

'When on earth did he have a chance to do that?'

'On the dance floor at The Lizard Lounge.'

'But it was so noisy in there.'

'I know. He sort of shouted it confidentially into my ear.'

'Silly old sod; but it's true,' admitted Lady A.

'Well, do you think you could do a bit of digging around for us, then, not just about the letter, but about the murder as well. It's going to be very detrimental to selling the other villas if the murderer isn't caught and put away. How can we possibly hope to shift – I mean, sell – all these lovely homes if there's a killer on the loose. It's bad enough having somebody killed in one of them, without the perpetrator running about loose all over the place.'

'I think I see what you mean,' replied Lady Amanda, working it out in her head, 'and of course we'll look into things: just don't let on to the others, or they'll all clam up and I won't be able to get a thing out of them.'

At Windy's agreement to this, there was the sound of jingling and clanking bottles, and Beauchamp came into view pulling two fully laden trolleys behind him, a big cheesy grin plastered across his face. 'You look happy,' commented Lady A.

'A beautiful wife and access to an absolute Aladdin's cave of drinks – how could I be anything

121

else?' he replied, and called over his shoulder, 'I'll be back for the rest when I've unpacked this lot.'

'The rest?' asked his employer.

'You, of all people, should know how many different ingredients are needed to give a real variety of cocktails. But the store here is even more extensive than yours. When we get back, there are a few bottles that I'd like to be purchased for consumption at Belchester Towers, if that's all right with you, your ladyship.'

'If you think we need ingredients, help yourself when we get back home. I'm hardly going to complain about you buying things that are going to make your creations even better, am I?'

Beauchamp dragged out the first of his booty with the face of one who has won one of life's little lotteries, and was celebrating his good fortune.

Chapter Ten

Windy had generously sent round her other staff in the shape of Marilyn, her house-keeper, and Dwayne and Royston, respectively houseboy and gardener, both dressed in their best suits, to help serve the drinks and canapés to the guests, and Beauchamp was having a fine time with lower ranks to order around. Apart from Enid's invaluable help, he was used to being a one-man band and, as far as comestibles were concerned, Maria was still there, too, and doing her best to help – interfere – with the canapés that Enid was making.

122

'Ah always put de caviar on de cream cheese wid de smoked salmon on top,' she offered.

Enid sighed in exasperation and explained that she had learnt to put the cream cheese on first, then the smoked salmon, then to use the caviar as a decoration on the top.

'You English sure is strange people,' judged Maria, earning her a severe scowl.

'I suppose you're going to have a go at my devils on horseback as well,' Enid asked in exasperation.

'No Ah ain't. Someone seems to have teached you to do dem right,' replied Maria, without a hint of irony or humour in her voice.

Enid proceeded to drop a huge bundle of asparagus tips into boiling water, and shooed Maria away, instructing her to make sure the table was ready for the platters of canapés, and that there were sufficient plates and napkins waiting for the guests.

Dwayne and Royston were employed in taking through jugs of ready-mixed margaritas and a large tray of ready-salted glasses, and Marilyn was uncorking bottles of red wine so that they had time to breathe before being poured. All was well, and it was nearly time for the frivolities to commence.

Hugo appeared in the hall in, amazingly, a white tuxedo – how on earth had he keep that quiet? – then Lady Amanda slowly descended the stairs in the most dazzling of kaftans that had yet been seen on the island, and proceeded to say, most annoyingly, 'Oh, this old thing? I had my seamstress run it up for me out of a spare bale of silk, before we came over.' What a deceitful old bunny she was, but she did look quite spectacular – all things considered, like her age, her figure...

Windy and Beep-Beep were the first to arrive, coming from just next door, and both exclaimed with approval and pleasure at how professional everything looked. 'Why, I don't think I've ever seen the staff so smartly attired, and someone's done some real magic with flowers.'

'That was Maria,' volunteered Hugo, who had taken to Maria, and felt that she should get full credit for going out with some stout secateurs, and hacking away at flowering trees and shrubs to provide the beautiful multi-coloured displays that now adorned the many side-tables.

'I should have known what she was up to when she mysteriously disappeared with almost all my vases,' replied Windy with a smile, helping herself to a margarita as she spoke. 'My, how delicious. The glass is just perfectly salted. You were right about Beauchamp being the best,' she exclaimed to Lady Amanda, who just smirked with satisfaction looking like the cat that had got the cream.

'And he's all mine,' she replied boastfully.

'Not quite,' piped up a voice, as Enid came into view with a silver platter of delicious nibbles. 'Some parts of him are definitely mine.'

Lady A made a little moue of distaste, and let her know that she could have those parts, as she wasn't in the least interested in what she referred to as 'the giblets', and Enid gave a snort of un-ladylike laughter at the description.

Then, there was a real run on the doorbell, as everyone seemed to arrive in one continuous stream. Although Eeyore's face was puffy and

124

blotchy, her eyes still red and swollen, she had made the effort of changing into a frock and applying some lipstick.

As everyone streamed in and hunted down or ordered their particular poison, the mood, although sombre and subdued at first, soon picked up a bit with the application of a couple of extra-lethal cocktails, and Lady Amanda and Hugo began to circulate.

Behind the makeshift bar of a decorating table swathed in white table cloths, Beauchamp did a number of skilful tricks with bottles and the cocktail shaker of which Lady Amanda had no idea he was capable, and just for a second or two, she could see Tom Cruise standing there – but as he was so much smaller, she let her mind shift back to Beauchamp, who was doing a sterling job keeping the old girls entertained. There was plenty of 'ooh-ing' and 'ah-ing' as he spun bottles in the air, catching them again with complete confidence, and what he did with his cocktail shaker was nobody's business.

Enid looked on from the food table, almost bursting with pride. She looked quite the new woman. Windy, who had just gone home to fetch her iPod and speakers, put on some lovely old music, and Hugo grabbed Lady Amanda and swung her into a waltz, to which the others responded with a round of applause.

Apart from Beauchamp, who was much too busy to bother with dancing, Beep-Beep was the only other man present, so there was a particularly bitchy competition to be his partner, and then the other girls reluctantly paired off, dancing as they had done in school, with each other.

The only one missing was Adonis, who suddenly appeared as the ghost at the feast in their midst; the music went off with as much rapidity as it had gone on, and the mood went down a notch or two. They hadn't had quite sufficient to drink yet to really make the party go with a swing, but they'd get there, given time. It was like a rehearsal for the dear departed Douglas's wake.

After a few more cocktails, however, the atmosphere started to lighten again. Enid, although she had worked really hard to make enough canapés, was enjoying the varied company enormously, after so long with just her new husband.

Said husband was also having a really good time. His specials for the evening were Caribbean Sunsets, cocktails with a glorious red band at the bottom of the glass, and Yellow Parrots, small but deadly, and they were going like hot cakes. As he mixed, he thought how grounded and secure he felt since he had married dear Enid. He felt that he would never have a recurrence of his irritating little problem when the red mist descended, for as long as he lived. He certainly hoped not, or it could ruin more lives than his own.

After a few bevvies, Wuffles had taken quite a shine to Hugo in his white DJ, and cornered him on a sofa for a little chat. She hadn't yet reached the embarrassingly flirty stage of inebriation, so he felt quite safe. After a few polite opening generalisations, she began to open up about how she and Longshanks had always been at loggerheads. 'In that way, we're very like Horseface and Fflageolet.

'We never got on from day one. There's just

something about her that rubs me up the wrong way. Maybe it's the fact that she looked like a dog we used to have when I was little that used to growl every time it saw me,' she confessed – she could talk; Hugo could hardly believe his ears, hearing this from a woman who herself looked uncannily like a spaniel – 'or maybe it's just because she's so small. Have you noticed how tiny she is? Even as a child she was undersized, and it was the source of quite a lot of bullying. Girls can be so cruel – much worse than boys.'

Hugo took as much as he could stand, and made his escape with the excuse of a trip to the little boys' room, before she went a stage further and started making eyes at him. By a sneaky detour, he managed to get himself to the kitchen, where the only occupant was Beep-Beep, no doubt having sought sanctuary from all the old girls, who were getting to the point of being in 'frisky' mode.

Beauchamp, ever watchful, slipped briefly into the room and handed each of them a glass, muttering, 'Yellow Bird, double size' before whisking back to his post at the makeshift bar. Beep-Beep raised his glass and took a long swallow.

'I don't suppose you and your lady-friend have given any thought to purchasing one of the villas?' he asked, a look of slight anxiety on his face.

'Not really, although she did say she'd consider it. Oh, and by the way, old man, she's not my lady-friend, not the way you mean. She's just a platonic friend from years ago, and she happens to be kind enough to let me live in her house – nothing dodgy about our relationship at all.'

'Didn't mean to offend, Hugo, but has she

mentioned whether she'd made any decision?'

'I think she'd like to do the viewing first. She makes up her mind quite quickly, but not before having seen the actual product.'

'Fair enough. I'll get Windy to organise it as soon as possible. We've got ten, you know, just sitting there, with occasional visitors, but we've got all that money tied up, and I reckon we've got to sell some of them soon, or we'll be stony broke.' Really! Those two next-door did nothing but moan about money and selling the properties. Surely they couldn't be that broke?

'No!' Hugo was shocked, considering their life-style. 'But this place with the pool? Your booze cupboard? You give the impression of being absolutely loaded.'

'Not so. It wouldn't do to give any other impression, but we're damned near on our uppers. Give Sniffy a gentle nudge, will you, please?'

It took Hugo a second or two to compute who Sniffy was, but when the penny dropped, he assured Beep-Beep that he would do that for him as soon as they were alone.

'Thanks, old man. Very grateful and all that; and any influence she might have over the other visitors would also be greatly accepted. Might even offer her a discount, if you can swing this one for us, and a wee bit extra, for everyone she persuades to buy one.'

Hugo left the kitchen as embarrassed as he had entered it, although for a different reason. He had really gone from the frying pan into the fire, with a choice between being made up to by a woman that looked like she belonged on the end of a lead, to that unmentionable subject, money. He was really uncomfortable discussing it, and the idea that Beep-Beep thought he had any influence whatsoever over Manda was laughable beyond belief, although he would tell her about the conversation, just because he had given his word that he would.

Lady Amanda, meanwhile, was having a bit of a shake with Windy, asking her if she'd had any idea yet who might have sent her the anonymous letter, and whether there had been any follow up. When the answer came back in the negative, she told Windy that she was going to disappear for a short time, and that, if anyone asked about her, she was to say that she was in the bathroom. That way, at least nobody would seriously come looking for her. Just before she slipped away, Windy asked her where she was going, but she just put a finger up to her lips, and eased herself out of the room.

Once outside, she grabbed the bottom of her silk kaftan, and raised it to knee level to allow herself more speed, and shot off into the garden of 12A, thinking that in her opinion, before they had arrived, the kaftan she had had specially modelled would be far too garish to be worn in public, but she had been proved wrong, and was really pleased with the opportunity to be able to wear such an eye-catching garment, but then, she had known where Enid was going for her honeymoon, which Enid had not.

Moving round to the back of the house and producing a penlight torch from her handbag, she approached the refuse bin and opened the lid. If someone had cut out the letters to make the words of the anonymous communication, then they would have ditched the periodicals or newspapers from which they had been cut. She was going to work her way round this side of the close, then work her way back to Cocktails via the other side.

In the garden of The Palms, number nine, she said a very rude word as she barked her right shin on a stone garden statue, and hoped that the sound didn't carry to anyone outside at the party. She didn't want her little investigative trip discovered and her cover blown this early in the investigation – investigations! There were definitely two of them now, but at present, she was engaged in finding the compiler of the anonymous letter.

Make that three, for she would dearly love to know what Windy's dark secret was. There had to be one or there would not have been a letter in the first place. What had she and Beep-Beep got to hide that couldn't be made public to her old chums? Rubbing her smarting leg, she moved on to the next occupied property.

Meanwhile, back at the party, Wuffles was in combative mood, and had, by now, button-holed Windy, and was challenging her about why she had to share a villa with Longshanks. She didn't mind Droopy-Drawers, who was also staying in the same villa: in fact, she wouldn't have minded anyone else, but surely Windy remembered how at daggers-drawn those two had always been at school.

'I'm terribly sorry, Wuffles, old stick, but I'd simply forgotten. It was so long ago that it had

130

completely slipped my mind,' she apologised. 'I'd forgotten the childish animosity about Horseface and Fflageolet as well, and look where that got me.'

'How on earth could you forget that dorm fight where we ended up bursting half a dozen pillows and ripping one mattress almost to shreds, as well as tearing out each other's hair? Or that scrap on the hockey pitch, where we gave each other simultaneous concussion with our sticks?'

'I can't imagine how I didn't remember those two events, but unfortunately, I forgot. If you'd like me to move you to an empty property, I'll be happy to do so, but I don't think I can disturb Longshanks, as she hasn't made any complaint.'

At this offer, Wuffles looked sulky, and said she would sleep on it and let her know the next day. 'I don't want to cause any bad feeling,' she muttered.

'I would have thought staying on in the same villa would have been more of a recipe for disaster,' opined Windy, and Wuffles shuffled away to get herself the solace of another of Beauchamp's excellent cocktails.

Windy sighed with relief, only to espy Fflageolet heading in her direction with a determined expression on her face. Oh, God, what now? she thought, and grabbed a glass of ready-mixed patience from the table to sustain her through her next ordeal.

Fflageolet, her emotions stirred up earlier by the murder of Adonis, had distracted herself by remembering Horseface's accusation of the theft of her diamond tennis bracelet. All this had done was get her temper up, and she was determined to have a damned good word with Windy, for although the ex-head girl had broken up the fight, she felt she was due an apology from somebody – anybody – but Windy was the nearest to her, and she'd do as well as anybody, the mood Fflageolet was in.

'You owe me an apology big time,' she said in a rasping voice, pointing a finger at Windy aggressively.

'Whatever for, Fflageolet? What have I done now?'

'It's what you haven't done. You came over and broke up that fight between me and Horseface, and you found her bracelet safe and sound, but I don't remember you saying sorry to me.'

'I had nothing to apologise for. It wasn't I who accused you of stealing anything,' replied Windy, retaining her dignity. 'I'm sure Horseface apologised very nicely when she realised she was in the wrong. Did she?'

Fflageolet's face was a mask of confusion. 'I can't ... I can't actually remember,' she stuttered.

'Bet she did. It's just the drink. Relax, enjoy yourself, and just let everything go for tonight,' Windy advised, and Fflageolet wandered aimlessly away towards the bar. The sound of swearing drifted through the open patio doors from some distance away, but Windy just assumed that it was some of the locals in horseplay.

Meanwhile, Hugo had been completely unaware of the lanky figure of Horseface creeping up on him, and it was only when she let a hand drop on to his shoulder that he knew there was anybody behind him. 'Dance, Hugs?' the figure enquired, and she grabbed Hugo and began to sway to the quiet strains of the old-fashioned wind-up gramophone player which Beep-Beep had started up in the back garden.

Hugo was too polite to refuse, but after what she asked him next, he wished he had done. 'How's your dribbly bum?' she asked forthrightly. 'I hear you had quite a time on the old latrine the other night.'

Blushing a bright shade of scarlet, Hugo explained rather haltingly that his problem was completely better, and that he would be grateful if she wouldn't mention it again, as the memory was still too vivid.

''S nothing to be ashamed of,' she continued, refusing to leave the situation alone. 'A lot of people suffer from a form of Delhi Belly when they go away to foreign climes. I've been quite loose myself, to be honest. You're certainly not on your own. Hey, everybody, Hugs's dribbly bum's better,' she concluded, raising her voice so that as many guests as possible could hear this important announcement.

Excusing himself as the tune ended and his embarrassment rose to crippling proportions, Hugo agreed that this was indeed so, and he removed himself so that he could be just that – alone and undisturbed for a while. He was of the opinion that some of the old girls were already the worse for wear, as far as cocktails were concerned, and it wasn't just his stomach that was easily upset.

Meanwhile, back in the rear gardens, Lady Amanda swore loudly again as she knocked over a dustbin. The light of her torch had just started to fail, and it had blinked out altogether for a few seconds; just long enough for her to stumble over the dustbin, sending both it and her sprawling on the grass.

'Bugger! Damn! Blast! *Merde!*' she finished, in French, thinking that swearing in another language wasn't so bad as swearing in one's parent tongue. Lady A then clapped a hand to her mouth, and listened intently to discern whether anyone had heard her incontinent language. All was quiet, however, so she inspected the contents of the bin she had knocked over which, fortunately, didn't include any messy food scraps, then moved on to the next one.

She didn't actually enter the garden of number seven, for from this close proximity, she could see a light moving inside number five, the villa Douglas Huddlestone-Black had been using, and she was quite sure that if the police wanted to search it at this time of the evening, they would not be doing so with a torch. There was someone in there who had no right to be and, as far as she knew, all the old girls were at the cocktail party at her and Hugo's place.

Making as little noise as possible, she began to creep closer and closer to the back gate, hoping that she could surprise whoever was in there, at the same time, hoping that she wouldn't, for there was no guarantee of a good outcome to the situation.

As she opened the back gate, she could see that the back door was not properly shut. She also heard the most awful screech from the hinges of the gate, and froze, lest her presence be detected. Immediately the torch, or whatever it was, was turned off in the interior of the villa. She heard the sound of the front door opening with some force, as it bumped back against the wall in the hall, then she heard footsteps disappearing away from the villa.

Feeling that it was now safe for her to enter, she did so, going straight to the open front door and seeing the silhouette of a tall figure just disappearing round the end of number one, the last house on this side. Who was it, and what had they been looking for?

It was the same figure she had seen watching the boat and the dinghy from the beach, and the same one she had seen disappearing into the undergrowth at the lagoon. She just could not put an identity to it. Were all the girls at her place, or had one of them slipped out, as she had done? The only one tall enough was Horseface, who wasn't exactly the most feminine of women and, in the dark, could easily be mistaken for a man. On the other hand, she was quite sure Horseface had been at the lagoon when she saw that furtive figure amongst the huge ferns that grew around its shoreline.

Her memory wasn't as exact as she would like, and she'd have to leave that thought to work away at itself while her mind was elsewhere. For the moment, she went round to the back of number one, but there was no sign of anyone. Now, Horseface lived in number one, so she might just look through the windows of that particular abode, to see if she had come back, but she could detect no movement or light inside, and was sure the place was unoccupied.

Going back to the garden of number five, she found a very large refuse container, and had to stand on a handy lump of stone to look inside it. It really was cavernous, she thought, as she bent her head, then the top of her body inside, trying to identify if there were any discarded newspapers or magazines in the bottom.

At that moment the garbage can literally ate her, as her centre of gravity shifted from outside the container to inside, and she tumbled in head first, pulling the thing over on its side as she went. Ah, so there had been something in there after all, she thought, as a certain stickiness made itself known at her midriff.

She crawled backwards to escape her prison and, having done so and put on her penlight, she found that the three old girls who were staying at number five must have had doggy bags from one of their meals out: doggy bags containing ribs in hot sauce. Her middle section was smeared with the stuff, one of the ribs actually sticking to the front of her immaculate silk kaftan.

With a snort of disgust, she picked it away, inserted it back in the bin and righted the bin, before deciding to abandon her task. Not only had she been away long enough from her party, but she urgently needed to change. She smelt hot and spicy, and could remain in her present state no longer without feeling slightly sick.

On the other hand, if she had a quick rummage through the refuse at number two, she would have finished this side, and that would only leave her with Cocktails itself, which she couldn't search, what with the party going on next door. Apart from where she and Hugo were staying, the only occupied villa on this side of the road was Beauchamp and Enid's, and she was sure those two hadn't had the time, let alone the knowledge, to send an anonymous letter to Windy.

Nothing suspicious discovered in the last bin of her investigative trip, Lady Amanda made her way back to number fifteen, wondering how she was going to explain the state of her kaftan to the others, who hadn't even known she'd slipped out, let alone why.

She was lucky, in that most of the party-goers had gone out into the garden to enjoy the nostalgic music and the tropical night air, and that Hugo, who had just come out of the downstairs facilities, saw her shape through the glass of the front door. Opening it, he looked at her aghast, and asked her what the heck she had been up to.

As Lady Amanda entered the hall and inhaled a large breath to explain her sticky and messy condition, Windy and Beep-Beep strolled back into the villa and saw her. She immediately made a ninety degree turn so that she was facing the wall, and answered their greeting from this position.

'What on earth are you doing, Sniffy?' asked Windy.

'I was ... I was ... just considering that this piece of wall would look good with a picture hanging from it,' she improvised, then sidled her way along the wall muttering. 'And here ... and here,' until she reached the foot of the staircase. 'Well, I just want to go up to my room to freshen up,' she declared boldly, and began to mount the staircase. Unfortunately, about five steps up, it turned sharply to the left, and she went up the remainder of the steps in a strange crab-like shuffle, keeping her front deliberately away from prying eyes.

'Are you all right, Sniffy?' called Windy after her, and Hugo put out a hand to restrain her from following.

'She'll be fine. She probably just needs to take one of her indigestion tablets. Alcohol sometimes does that to her.' Hugo was quite good at making up stories too, but he'd have to remember to tell Manda that she took the medication when he got the chance to speak to her again in private.

Gently he guided Windy and Beep-Beep back to the heart of the party, and snuck back to the hall to see if Manda had come down yet. He found her just arriving back on the ground floor, now wearing a locally-bought kaftan, with no sign of the filthy silk she had arrived in at the front door.

'What on earth had happened to you?' asked Hugo, determined to get the truth out of her.

'I just had a run-in with the contents of a dustbin,' she whispered, looking from side to side to see if anyone could overhear her. 'Wait till everybody's gone, and I'll fill you in on the details.' And with this, he had to be content for now. She was evidently not going to spill even one bean while everyone else was in the house.

Although some of the old girls remarked on her change of kaftan, they were in such a state of relaxation by now that they merely took it as normal that she should change mid-party, and for this, she was relieved. Only Windy went that little bit further, and fixed her with a steely gaze of interrogation. 'I'll tell you later,' Lady A hissed at her in an undertone, and wafted off majestically like a proud galleon in full-sail.

The first to leave was Fflageolet. So small was her build that she was easily carried home by Horseface, dead to the world, drowned in a sea of alcohol. Longshanks wasn't long behind her, carried by her arms and legs like an upturned turtle by Wuffles and Droopy-Drawers. They'd feel awful in the morning, but nothing that couldn't be cured by a hair of the dog that bit them and a damned good fry-up.

The others dribbled off in ones and twos, and soon, only Windy and Beep-Beep, Beauchamp and Enid, and Lady Amanda and Hugo remained, and Beauchamp shut the open patio doors to keep out any more insects than had already joined them for a feast on very well-hung meat.

The six of them settled down in the sitting room, the ladies with a Yellow Parrot each, the gentlemen with Caribbean Sunsets to hand, and Windy felt bold enough to ask, in this reduced company, why Lady Amanda had acted so strangely in the hall and on the stairs, and why she had changed her kaftan.

She explained about her investigations in the gardens, drawing sympathy for her barked shin, and horror that she had entered a house which probably contained Adonis' murderer. Having told them that the place was in even more of a state than it had been when they had gone there to view the newly discovered corpse, she gave her opinion that someone was looking for something that they hadn't found yet, and reiterated her recollections of having seen the tall figure before, but not being able to place exactly who it was.

When she got to the part of the story where she fell into a bin, they all hooted with laughter, and were most unkind about her hot sauce-stained kaftan. 'I'll bet you haven't looked so hot or smelt so seductive in years,' commented Beep-Beep, earning himself a savage scowl. Beauchamp cleared his throat in embarrassment at this uncalled for and insulting remark, and knew that Lady Amanda would, somehow, get her own back on him.

'Will we be going round for viewings tomorrow, then?' asked Lady Amanda, out of the blue, and Hugo spiked her with an inquisitive eye. She was up to something; he was sure of it.

'I expect we'll be bothered by the police in the morning, but I see no reason why we can't go round them in the afternoon. Beep-Beep and I will lead separate parties, so that there aren't too many of us in one house at any time. I'll give you a tinkle about the timing,' replied Windy.

'Could you be sure and put Hugo and me in the second group, and Beauchamp and Enid in the first?' she asked.

'Of course. I'm sure you have your reasons,' Windy responded, hoping that these would be revealed, but no dice there, though.

'Oh, I do. And I should like us to look at all of the villas: even the ones the girls are staying in. I expect they'll all want to look in this one, and we don't mind, do we Hugo?'

'Uh?' Hugo hadn't been paying attention.

'We won't mind if the girls all look round this villa if they're viewing tomorrow, will we?'

'Er, no,' he muttered, thinking that he'd have to make sure there was no way they could go through his underwear. He wouldn't put it past them, so he'd better lock personal items like that in his suitcase and make sure he had the key with him, when they were going round.

'Do you remember that girl, Fiona, with the braces and the waist-length hair at school?' asked Windy, the final drink of the evening suddenly making her come over all nostalgic.

'I believe I do,' replied Lady A. 'What about her?'

'Did you ever hear the story of her baby blankets and the nanny?'

'No. Go on.'

Windy started to chuckle as she remembered. 'When she was born, her mother did her best for family politics. As she had had a girl, she called her Fiona after her own mother, with the middle name Olivia, after her mother in-law, but she completely disregarded her married name. Do you remember the family name, Sniffy?'

'Finlay-Finch, if my memory serves me correctly,' replied Lady A, with a small smirk of triumph. 'What about it?'

'Her mother only went and had the kid's initials embroidered on the top right-hand corner of all her pram blankets, and when Nanny saw the child all tucked up in her perambulator with that sewn on, she fainted away, and had to be roused with smelling salts.'

'Why?' asked Hugo, who still wasn't giving the

conversation his full attention, as it was well past his usual bedtime.

'Her mother had had her initials embroidered on her pram blankets, Hugo,' explained Windy slowly and carefully, 'and her name was Fiona Olivia Finlay-Finch. Just think of the initials.'

Hugo's ears went pink, as realisation dawned, and he said, 'Didn't her mother notice?'

'She had led too much of a sheltered childhood to realise what it meant,' said Windy, finally driving home the final nail in the coffin of what she had considered a quick and amusing little story. Hugo had certainly put paid to that.

When it was just the two of them again, Hugo asked her what she intended to do on these proposed viewings. 'I'm going to hang around at the back of the group, especially in those properties that are occupied at the moment, and have a little riffle through their pedal bins, or wherever they put their domestic rubbish. I'm also going to go out into all the back gardens again and see if I can see signs of anyone having burnt anything. In my opinion, that would be the sensible thing to do with any newspapers or periodicals from which letters had been cut.'

Chapter Eleven

Lady Amanda had established a routine with Maria that she and Hugo be served tea in bed at eight-thirty, but today this happy routine was interrupted. DI Pharaoh had returned to the area with Sergeant Waladii, and the two of them made an early raid on those they wanted to talk to in the Parrot Bay properties.

Thus it was, that they knocked rather vigorously on the door of number fifteen at eight o'clock, and Maria called loudly upstairs from the hall. 'Lady Amanda, Mr Hugo, we got a policeman on de doorstep. What you want I should do wid him?'

Hugo was difficult to rouse from his slumbers, but Lady Amanda was suddenly wide awake, and called back. 'Put him in the sitting room, and Hugo and I will be down as soon as we've made ourselves decent.'

Pulling on a light but long dressing gown, she went into Hugo's room and began the delicate process of waking him up. She grabbed him by the shoulders and started to shake him gently at first, then with more vigour. Hugo puffed and snorted and stirred, so Lady A decided it was time for stage two of this particular operation. Leaning close to his face, she continued to shake him, but added to this a loud repetition of his name. 'Hu-go. Hu-go. Wake up. Wake up, damn you! There's a *policeman* waiting downstairs to talk to us.'

143

Letting go of his shoulders, she began to slap his cheeks lightly. 'Hu-go, police.' Grabbing his shoulders once more and giving him a much more vigorous shake, she shouted one final time, but much louder. 'Hugo! Police.'

'Wassup? Whassgoinon? Wurra-wurra-wurra wot,' he babbled as consciousness slowly returned. 'Wha' you doin' in my room, Manda?'

'You have to get out of bed now and come downstairs.'

'But I haven't had my early morning tea yet,' he said, this vital fact suddenly striking him. 'Where's Maria got to?'

'It's only just gone eight o'clock, Hugo, and Maria hasn't brought our tea yet.'

Hugo flung himself back into his sleeping position and attempted to return to the land of slumber, but Lady Amanda wasn't standing for mutiny like that. 'Hugo, there's a policeman downstairs who wants to talk to us – NOW! Wake up! You have to get out of bed.'

'Must I?' he whined, lifting a pathetic face to his house-mate.

'Yes you must. This isn't a good old British bobby. This is a foreign policeman, and he might clap you in irons for not co-operating. Come on, now, put your dressing gown on and come down with me, and we can have our tea when he's gone.'

This threat was enough to convince Sleeping Beauty that he really did have to get out of his bed, but before he came out from under the covers, he said, 'Would you mind turning round first, Manda. I don't like to be seen in my pyjamas, especially not by someone of the female persuasion.'

'Hugo, it's me, Manda,' she replied, slightly hurt, but complying with his request. 'How can you possibly class me as one of those silly women?'

'Because, technically, you are one.'

'Stuff and nonsense. Now hurry up, or he'll get restive, and then Lord knows what he'll do to us. I for one don't fancy being handcuffed and hauled off to whatever passes for the local clink on this island.'

It took ten minutes to get Hugo sufficiently awake to put on his dressing gown, then he insisted on brushing his thick white hair before he could be seen in public. When he'd first gone to prep school, he'd been known as Haystack for a while, and it was a nickname he didn't fancy being revived.

Maria was waiting for them in the hall, wringing her hands together. 'You'd better hurry you'selves up. Ah think he's getting fed up of waitin' for you.'

With this in mind, Lady Amanda swept majestically into the sitting room and held out her right hand. 'Lady Amanda Golightly,' she enunciated slowly and clearly. The man had to know exactly with whom he was dealing, here. 'And my friend Mr Hugo Cholmondley-Crichton-Crump.' She held out a hand to indicate the shy and retiring figure standing behind her. Let him chew on that for a minute or two, and see how hungry he still felt.

DI Pharaoh had sent Sergeant Waladii to visit the old girls who were staying on the close, but not actually been instrumental in discovering the body, reserving this house and Cocktails, next door, for himself. He didn't mind handing out scraps to those of inferior rank, but he liked to keep the real meat for himself. This analogy came into his head as he decided that Lady Amanda had the early morning face of a disgruntled bull-dog, and it was only early by her undisciplined standards. He was up every morning at five thirty so that he could go for a run before breakfasting and going into the station.

'I wonder if you could tell me about the events of yesterday morning when you two and, I believe, one of your next door neighbours, discovered the body of Mr Douglas Huddlestone-Black.' He had come over from the mainland again, and there was a definite American twang to his accent.

'There's not much to tell, actually. Windy – I mean Wendy – from next door at Cocktails...' – she did not provide a surname, because she wasn't sure whether Windy had retained her maiden name, or had changed it on marrying Beep-Beep – came to our door yelling her head off, and seemed very shocked and upset by something, didn't she, Hugo?' She finished with this question, because she wanted Hugo to at least join in the explanation, even if it was just agreeing with what she said.

'She was hysterical,' replied Hugo, exceeding all her expectations. 'And we offered to go to see whatever it was that had upset her.'

'And that was?' DI Pharaoh decided to get at least three words in edgeways.

'Well, Douglas was supposed to be going to the next island to catch a flight home, and she hadn't seen him leave. Usually he dropped the keys to the villa into her mailbox...'

'Cut to the chase, lady,' instructed the inspector.

Bridling at such a rude interruption, Lady Amanda continued her tale. 'But the keys never appeared, so she went over to number five with her spare key to see if everything was alright. When she came across the dead body of Mr Huddlestone-Black, she came straight over here and asked us to go back with her, just to confirm that she hadn't misinterpreted what she had seen.

'This we did. We discovered his suitcases in the hall, with the contents strewn everywhere. Win ... Wendy led us upstairs to the room he slept in, and there he was, lying on the floor with his throat cut.'

'Can you confirm this, Mr Chumley ... Umley ... Um ... sir?'

'Indeed I can,' replied Hugo. 'It was like a horrible, bloody smile, from ear to ear. Most upsetting for the ladies – and for me, as well,' he added, screwing up his face in disgust at the memory.

'Have you any theories as to who could have been responsible for his murder, or why he was killed?'

'Absolutely none, Inspector. Neither of us knows a thing, nor have we been on the island long enough for us to know who Mr Huddlestone-Black knew here. He wasn't exactly what you'd call the sociable type, and kept very much to himself.' She had decided not to mention seeing him in the jewellery quarter the other day.

'And you, Mr Ch ... sir?'

'Not a clue, old boy,' replied Hugo, innocence shining out of his face.

Not quite sure whether the term 'old boy' was a friendly term, or whether it was a slur on his age, the inspector took his leave of them, informing them that he would be calling next door at Cocktails to see if the lady there confirmed their statements.

He was much longer interviewing Windy, who broke into hysterical sobs as soon as he entered the house. It took quite some time for her to tell her version of what had happened, punctuated, as it was, with sobs, nose-blowing, eye-wiping, hiccoughs, and frequent pathetic appeals to Beep-Beep to make it all go away.

When Pharaoh finally found himself outside the house, he discovered that Sergeant Waladii had finished all the visits he had needed to make, and was leaning against the trunk of a tree enjoying the shade. 'We ought to get back,' he stated baldly. 'They said the results of the autopsy would be available this morning, so I suggest we go back to the security force's offices and radio in.'

'They might have turned up something that wasn't immediately obvious, I suppose,' mused the inspector.

'And piggies might fly. Do we really have to stay in that ramshackle old house they've found for us?'

'Damned right we do, until we can take back the person responsible for this killing.'

'Holy Moses!' Sergeant Waladii wasn't at all impressed.

Windy had finally recovered herself sufficiently to make two lists of old girls for viewing the properties. She had been a little surprised that Lady Amanda wanted to see all of the villas, but she probably wanted to see what they could look

like when someone had stamped some personality on them.

Even the ones that were only being stayed in
were still for sale, and she thought the few who
lived there wouldn't be in the least discomposed at
letting their friends see how they had personalised
the blank canvases they had purchased and, to be
fair, each and every one of the dwellings was very
slightly different in design and execution from its
neighbours anyway.

The first group assembled at one thirty, missing
nobody – as everyone, given the chance, loves
looking round other people's homes, so that they
can be catty about them afterwards. This was the
group that Beep-Beep would take round, and as
soon as he left, Windy drifted round to see her
old ink monitor.

When Hugo answered the door to her, she
hustled past him until she found Lady Amanda,
still in the kitchen finishing her lunch. Without
preamble, she plunged into her first question.
'You didn't tell him anything other than what
we'd agreed, did you, Sniffy?'

'Of course I didn't, Windy. What do you take
me for? A fool?'

'And you didn't mention that we had a bit of a
poke around before I locked the place back up?'

'My lips are sealed. What are you so worried
about? Do you think it might have been Adonis
who sent you that letter?'

'No, of course I don't. I just don't want to be
caught out with a question I'm not prepared for.
I might really put my foot in it.'

'Have a glass of mango juice and stop being
149

such a worry-guts. They'll find out who did it, and then life will just get back to normal.'

'Do you really think so, Sniffy?'

'Of course I do. You know we've got experience of this sort of thing and I can assure that it will seem like no time at all before we're all wondering what all the fuss was about,' Lady Amanda reassured her.

'A man was killed,' stated Windy defiantly.

'He was, but not a man any of us ever knew well, or was really close to. You'd be surprised how a ripple in a pond, no matter how far the rings spread out, is soon dispersed by the sheer weight of the rest of the water. Don't fret so. Everything will be fine, you'll see.'

Windy didn't look convinced, but went back next door for a quick snifter before she too had to traipse round all their properties, being Ms Enthusiastic Guide. She and Beep-Beep were gutted that the properties hadn't sold quicker, but you've got to play the hand you're dealt, and if she could unload a couple on these old school-friends, they'd be back on more secure ground. For now.

The second group of viewers set out at two-thirty. The arrangement was for Beep-Beep to unlock the properties and leave them so, so that the second group could follow on not far behind. That way, the proceedings shouldn't take an enormous amount of time, and he could go back behind the second group locking up again.

Windy made them start at number one where Horseface and Fflageolet were staying but, as they had been in the first group, they weren't there to hear any disparaging comments made about the untidiness of their bedrooms and the number of items left to languish on a coffee table in the middle of the seating group in the living room.

As they left to move on to number two, Hop-along's year-round home, Windy realised that she'd lost Lady A. Hugo pleaded ignorance of her whereabouts, and she eventually found her in the kitchen going through the pedal bin. 'Whatever are you doing, Sniffy, going through the kitchen waste?' she asked, perplexed.

'The same as I was doing last night,' replied Lady Amanda haughtily. 'I'd have thought you would have guessed that I'm still on the trail of any magazines or newspapers that have letters or words cut out of them.'

'Gotcha! Good idea. I'll just leave you to trail along at the rear then, shall I?'

'As long as Beep-Beep doesn't lock me in somewhere in his enthusiasm to finish the task.'

'I know you: you'd soon make yourself heard.'

As she left her old chum to her own devices, happy that she was still looking into who had sent that wretched letter, Lady Amanda fell further and further behind the group, and when she finally got to number five, where Adonis had been staying, she noticed that the police crime scene tape had been removed, and the front door stood wide open.

Just before she reached the door, something nestling in a bushy shrub just to the right of the front door caught her eye. Bending down, she found a small suede bag complete with draw-strings to close it. Picking it up absently, she put it in her handbag to consider later. She needed to have a look in the deceased's bin in case he had been the one who had concocted the anonymous communication, but with no results.

More prepared for what she might find this time, she had brought a pair of thin rubber gloves, which she donned on entering each kitchen. These bins were much smaller than their exterior counterparts, but she didn't want to end up with filthy, stinky hands, and have everyone ask her what on earth she had been doing.

In number seven there were a number of waste-paper baskets to be looked through and, in one of the bedrooms, she came across a piece of paper that had been screwed up into a tight ball, after being torn up. Carefully reconstructing the sheet, she read at the top of it 'HM Customs & Excise', and her mind started to race. What was going on in this house? Was one of the occupants a smuggler? Somehow she couldn't see Wuffles, Droopy-Drawers, or Longshanks being involved with anything so underhand.

Another bin yielded another piece of discarded paper with the words, 'Meet me at midnight. Place as arranged' scrawled on it. Another mystery. Had one of these three ageing ladies found themselves a local beau? Another bag of waste had been put out by the refuse bin since last night and, keeping crouched down low, she rifled through this, only to come across some thin slivers of paper which could be off-cuts from someone compiling a rather nasty letter. The police obviously hadn't searched the house very closely.

There were no magazines or newspapers, but there was a small pile of ash at the very end of the garden that she had missed the evening before, that could indicate that someone had, perhaps burnt something incriminating. Could there be an innocent explanation for all she'd found. It seemed unlikely.

Had someone just burnt some rubbish that was too bulky for the bin? Who was being met at midnight, where and which night? How did the Customs people fit into things? These and other questions would need some thinking about, and she resolved not to engage in this activity until she was alone in her room at bedtime. She could discuss everything with Hugo, when they were both fresh in the morning, for she believed that Windy had plans that would use up the rest of their day.

Putting on a bit of a spurt, she missed out number eight – Beauchamp and Enid – and numbers ten and twelve that were empty, and hurried on to number fourteen, to which Eeyore had not yet returned. She would leave Cocktails until last, so that if she was caught wandering around, she could, untruthfully, plead that she had just been having a look round. She was determined to get to the bottom of why those two received that letter in the first place. They must be hiding something, or it would never have been sent at all. Someone had got something on them, and she wanted to know what that something was.

Once there, and after taking a quick peek out of the front window to see that no one was coming, she began to sort through the desk that sat at the back of the room, accidentally on purpose uncovering a bank statement, a letter in a foreign language, and a draft lease, and the contents of these two documents nearly made her hair stand on end. No! Surely not! Her lips clamped tight shut in disapproval, she made her way next door, where Hugo was just arriving, having given up on the last few villas. He'd had enough, and he wanted a cup of tea more than anything else in the world.

The old girls had just settled down in their villas to have some tea when there was the roar of an old engine and Winstone Churchill drove into Parrot Bay in a taxi that was in no better shape than his decaying old bus. Sounding the horn furiously, everyone came out to see what on earth had happened. Had war been declared, or had there been an outbreak of bubonic plague in the Caribbean?

He got out of the taxi and called them altogether, his face serious for the first time since they had met him. 'Ah got news for you,' he began. 'Momentous news. You know dat man who got hisself killed? Well, Ah just heard the result of the autopsy. His insides was brimful of emeralds. He was a smuggler, and dat's de truth.'

A babble of conversation broke out, as all Huddlestone-Black's secret and not-so-secret admirers began to question Winstone. It must be a rumour. He would never do a thing like that. Who had told him? Who would try to put a slur on dear Adonis' character like that?

Lady Amanda merely stood in silence, letting the hubbub wash over her. That was the answer to what had been in the empty suede bag she had found outside number five. That explained why he had been into that classy jeweller's – to get instructions about delivery from that 'yacht in the night'. That also explained why he had planned to go home when he did. He must have only just swallowed the stones. And he'd been coming out here two or three times a year. How many times had he smuggled back emeralds in his stomach? That was an awful lot of gems, and probably a whole heap of money going into his back pocket.

But it still didn't give her a clue to who had bumped him off. That was the biggest mystery of them all. Granted, she had uncovered a few other mysteries this afternoon, but this was the biggest puzzle that, at the moment, she didn't have a hope of solving.

Returning to the things she had found in the waste-paper bins in number six, she looked around to locate the three women who were staying there, but there was no sign of guilt on any of their faces. If one of them was a smuggler, maybe they had been in on it together, although what he would need an accomplice for she couldn't think.

Finally, Windy clapped her hands and yelled for silence and, given her former position of power over them, she was instantly obeyed. 'This has given us a lot of food for thought,' she said in a carrying voice. 'Thank God his poor Mother isn't alive to witness all this scandal.' A murmur of agreement went round, and she continued, 'I think that, after we've all had a bite of something to eat, we should meet outside number two and take a stroll down to the Beach Bar, where we can discuss this over a drink or two. We won't be overheard if we sit outside.'

Chapter Twelve

It was a subdued group of elderly women that gathered on the shore side of Coconut Corner an hour or so later, with the addition, of course, of Hugo and Beep-Beep. They were Beauchamp-less at the moment, as the couple had taken a rather cosy siesta after the exertions of house-viewing, and they were only just leaving number eight as the group moved the short distance to Old Uncle Obediah's Rum Keg Landing Beach Bar.

As they neared, a terrible sight met their eyes. There was no Short John Silver, but a pair of legs protruded on the sand from behind the bar itself. There were several squeals of dismay, and the old elderly party began to move as swiftly as they could towards the legs to see what had happened to the bar's proprietor.

Now, old people aren't very fast runners, and before they reached the scene of what they believed to be another dastardly deed, a short figure shuffling on its knees appeared from behind the counter, picked up the legs, and made off swifter than his visitors inside the shack that comprised the indoor area of the establishment.

Even as Beauchamp and Enid caught up with them and overtook them, Short John had been inside for a minute or two, the sand hampering what agility the others may still have possessed. As they all arrived, forming a clump round the entrance and peering into the gloom of the interior, they spotted the owner sitting on the floor, just beginning to strap on his prosthetic legs.

'Whatever were you doing with your legs left outside like that in the sun?' asked Windy, quite shrill with the apprehension she had felt at the sight.

'Ah just put dem out dere for dem to get a bit of colour. Dey're very pale, or hadn't you noticed?' he replied, with a straight face.

'Don't be so ridiculous. How could false legs ever catch the sun?'

'De magic of de tropics, of course.'

'That's just not good enough. You'll have to do better than that, John,' retorted Windy to this ridiculous claim.

For a moment there was complete silence, then the man finished fastening the last buckle and said, 'Look sometimes mah stumps get red raw wid the friction, and Ah need a bit of a rest from dem. Dat do you?'

Another second or two of silence ensued, before Windy said, 'I'm so sorry, John. I didn't mean to embarrass you, and you probably weren't expecting customers this early.'

'You right dere, Missus.' Short John hauled himself to his feet with the help of a chair. 'But how was you expected to know?'

'I should have thought about it more. They must become very uncomfortable in the heat. Please accept my sincere apologies.'

'No worries. Now, what can I get you delightful people to drink?'

'Blue Lagoons?' said Beep-Beep, interrogatively,

and there was a murmur of agreement. 'We're going to sit out here to catch the last of the sun, if you don't mind,' adding silently, 'where you can't eavesdrop on our conversation.'

Short John didn't mind where they sat, as long as they purchased plenty of drinks, and he started to pull bottles and glasses from one of the shelves behind the bar. 'You heard about dat autopsy? That man's gut was stuffed with gemstones.'

They all turned his way to see if he had any further information. 'Ah knowed he was up to no good. Ah seen him once, goin' out in a little dinghy to meet a boat. He was a bad one, dat Huddlestone-Black.'

'When was that?' asked Lady A with great interest.

'Can't remember. Sorry, lady, but all days is de same to me.'

Now she was confused. She'd seen a man looking, with binoculars, she thought, watching Adonis' activities the night she went out for a late walk, but it couldn't have been Short John. He wasn't very tall with his legs on, and even shorter with them off. Who else had been watching, and was it even the same night she was thinking of? And, come to that, who else was tall enough to have been that suspicious person? Surely it couldn't have been Horseface? She'd already dismissed this possibility, as the woman had been at the lagoon with the rest of them the day the figure had disappeared furtively into the undergrowth? She was certainly the right height, though. Bother!

'You're very quiet, Manda,' commented Hugo.

She gave him a blank stare, then collected her

scattered wits and replied, 'Just thinking about things, that's all, old stick. Nothing to worry about.' He seemed content with this, and returned to the slim straw in his glass, sucking at it with obvious enjoyment.

Lady Amanda returned to her deep thought. Very recently she had seen something that was out of kilter, but she couldn't for the life of her think what it was. Like crossword puzzle answers, though, she was sure it would come to her, but she was impatient to retrieve it from her memory.

She kept out of the conversation as the others discussed who might have been the murderer of dear old Adonis, and was still very quiet as they walked back to the villas in the dying rays of the sun, but Hugo was bursting with news. Back at the bar, he had been bursting with something quite different, and made his way out through the back of the shack to the primitive lavatories. In the back lobby he had come across Short John in earnest conversation with the tall figure of Horseface, and he happened, quite by accident to hear the tail-end of their conversation.

'But why have we got to wait till tomorrow night? Why not now?' the subdued, but still carrying, deep tones of Horseface asked.

'Because I'm just not ready yet. Don't rush me,' replied Short John, then broke off as he became aware of Hugo's presence.

As tall as Horseface was, they made an ill-matched couple, as Short John had those stubby prosthetic legs and so their height difference was quite noticeable. It was only as they left the bar that Hugo began to wonder about those two.

They seemed very friendly. He remembered them slipping away when they had last been here, to have a private chat. Was there anything in this strange relationship? He'd have to tell Manda as soon as they got back.

Just before they entered the close, Windy announced plans for them to visit one of the adjacent islands the next day for a jeep tour round it. She had decided it would be good to show them just how tatty and unkempt – uncivilised, she thought it – some of the other islands were, compared to Caribbaya. She'd done her best to sell the idea of buying a villa for either permanent or holiday enjoyment. Now she had to reinforce just how beautiful this island actually was.

The next morning, Winstone turned up in his rickety old bus to take them to the ferry landing stage just south of the cruise terminal, and they wandered out of the villas to board, some of them quite excited to get the chance to visit an adjacent island with which to compare Caribbaya. Hugo and Lady Amanda went right to the back of the bus, because they could talk more privately there, and Hugo had remembered that he still hadn't told Manda about what he'd overheard the previous evening, when he was on his way to the little boys' room at Old Uncle Obediah's Rum Keg Landing Beach Bar.

After regaling her with his little bit of gossip, he ended with, 'Do you really think they had an assignation for a bit of ... er ... hanky-panky?' Even the thought of it made Hugo flush pink.

'It easily could have been,' she replied thoughtfully, 'but it could be something quite different.'

At that point in their cogitations, Wuffles shuffled unsteadily along the, thankfully empty, aisle of the bus and plonked herself down in the seat in front of them. 'Sorry to interrupt,' she apologised, 'but Windy said it was alright to confide in you, as I did in her.'

This sounded very interesting, and the two occupants of the long back seat went completely quiet, and assumed interested expressions. Wuffles continued, now she could see she had their full attention, but kept her voice low, to that it would not carry to the front of the bus, even though it was unlikely to be heard there, as the other girls had started singing 'Ten Green Bottles' very lustily.

'I need to tell you that I'm actually on the island undercover. I used to work for HM Customs and Excise, and they called me out of retirement when I confided to a friend who still works there that I was coming out here.'

Lady Amanda and Hugo gave discreet gasps of surprise, and something fell into place in Lady A's brain. 'I thought you might be a smuggler yourself,' she admitted.

'Why on earth should you come to that conclusion?' Wuffles' canine face looked more hangdog than they thought possible.

'Because of a certain piece of paper screwed up into a ball with the department's name at the top, and a screwed up note that was arranging a midnight meeting with someone, although not the date or place,' admitted Lady Amanda.

'You've been going round hunting through bins

and waste-paper baskets, haven't you?'

'You bet, but that's enough of that for the moment. Tell us more.'

'The Department already had its suspicions about our Darling Douglas for a variety of reasons, and I was asked to keep an eye on him while I was out here, and to report on him if I had anything concrete. Well, of course, that's all up the spout now...'

'But I don't think you know everything that we know,' Lady A interrupted, and told Wuffles about her suspicions about Adonis and what he had actually done to his cabin steward. Also she told her about seeing him sneaking out of a shop in the jewellery district looking very furtive when he was supposed to be back at his villa.

'I'll certainly pass that on and get the steward's name checked out. What was he called? I knew someone was going on about having a different cabin steward, but I didn't think anything of it.'

'Sam, as far as I can remember. He also did one of the girl's cabins. It may have been Fflageolet's. You'll just have to ask.'

'I won't need to as I can give them the date of sailing, the name of the ship, and the first name of the steward, and that he had been responsible for Adonis's cabin. That should be enough to identify him, although what good it will do now, I don't know, except, perhaps to wrap up the case – sort of closing the stable door after the horse has bolted. Now, whoever is in on this gem-smuggling lark will just have to wait until someone else is appointed to take his place.

'If I follow my instincts, though, there's something else going on here, and that's why I decided not to go back just yet. I don't know who that note you found was to or from, but as I found it on the edge of our lawn, I shall presume it's one of the other two in my house. I shall be on guard every night, now, to see if either of them goes out just before the witching hour. There's something afoot, and I wouldn't mind betting it's something to do with smuggling. Did you smell that hashish the night we did the conga?'

'Sure did,' agreed Hugo, who was the one of the pair to identify it, much to Lady A's amazement.

'That was proof positive that it was getting on to the island, and I'm damned sure it's getting off it again for distribution in Europe. The only thing I don't know is how, and with whom. Will you keep your eyes peeled for me, and pass on anything you think suspicious?'

'Of course we will, Wuffles,' confirmed Lady A. 'By the way, where did you get hold of that midnight meeting letter, if it wasn't sent to you?' She'd said nothing about any of the other finds she had made at number seven. She liked to keep something up her sleeve.

'I told you just now. I found it crumpled up on the ground outside in the close, as if someone had pulled it out of their pocket by accident. Senior moment, or what?'

'And you're doing all this after you've officially retired, even though you've got a phobia about insects?'

'I'm just passionately anti-smuggling, and anyway, I was getting a bit bored.'

When she had gone, Lady Amanda confirmed

with Hugo that he actually believed her story, then said very quietly to him. 'I'm sure if Windy had told her about the anonymous letter she would have mentioned it. I'm certainly going to say nothing about that angle of what's going on here until she says something, or Windy gives me permission to spill the beans, as it were.'

'Discretion is our watchword,' said Hugo in agreement.

When the bus disgorged the flow of chattering old ladies at the south landing stage – plus Hugo and Beauchamp, as Beep-Beep had elected to stay behind and catch up with paperwork today – they were dismayed to find that the ferry was as rickety as the island's bus and taxi.

'Just how long are we going to be aboard this old tub?' Lady A didn't bother with polite niceties. She just got straight to the nub of the matter.

'The trip's about forty-five minutes there, and the same back,' replied Windy, indignantly. She could not encourage negative remarks of this kind, or she'd never shift those villas.

'Do you think it can stay afloat that long?'

'Don't be ridiculous: of course it can. It's perfectly seaworthy, if in need of a lick of paint,' she said, with a glower.

'And Ah plans to do just dat ting next week, Miz Windy,' called a musical voice from aboard the vessel, and a head of tightly curled hair looked out at them standing at the end of the landing stage. It was the kind of thing he always said when he had no real intention of doing something. The rest of the man followed, and he disembarked and came over to meet them.

Windy shot him a dazzling smile of welcome, and announced, 'Everybody, this is our ferryman for today, and he rejoices in the name Goodluck Johnston.' With little squeaks of amusement, the boating-party members shook hands and introduced themselves, as he helped them on to the ancient ferry.

'This should be a real hoot,' said Lady A, landing rather heavily in the ferry, and needing both Goodluck Johnston's hand and that of Beauchamp to help her to one of the bench seats that went round the sides of the craft. The weather was on the change, and there was a discernible swell on the way over, resulting in quite a few green faces and very little conversation. Those that were affected on the small craft shrunk in on themselves, entering their own private world of internal misery.

It was a relief when the ferry docked at the next island, as those who hadn't been upset by the sea's movement had been unsettled by the obvious suffering of those who had. They were met by a guide who was in charge of two jeeps with bench seating along the sides of the open back – the same as had been used for their previous trip through the jungly bit of Caribbaya, but these two vehicles looked like they were also on their last legs, and the bench seats felt unstable. The wood which had been used to make them was now splintered and split in its old age, so that there were quite a few complaints about getting either scratched or stabbed before the trip even began.

The jeeps set off with both drivers pointing out things of interest, which proved to be few and far between. After a few hundred metres, the metalled road leading from the dock turned into a dirt track, deeply rutted from the traffic that regularly used it. As there had been no rain for some time, the journey was doubly uncomfortable, as they were thrown around as well as being attacked by the spikiness of their rickety seats.

There were dilapidated gatherings of wooden buildings, outside which scrawny chickens scratched for food, and once a goat, which lunged as they approached, but was fortunately tethered and so just unable to deliver either a bite or a butt to those merely passing through.

Scantily-clad children ran outside of these ramshackle homes to wave at them and call out cheerful hellos, but the main township, when they reached it, was in poor condition too, and the lunch they stopped for at a makeshift restaurant offered only goat or chicken stew, which were cooked as well as they could be with limited ingredients. Lady Amanda whispered to Hugo that she thought this place hardly ever had many customers, and the cook simply didn't have the experience for what their group represented – mass catering.

'It's certainly not as pretty as where we're staying, although everyone seems friendly enough,' replied Hugo, smiling at the woman who was delivering large chunks of bread, torn by hand, from a much larger loaf made with a strong wholemeal flour.

After lunch, they were served with cold, weak coffee in enamel mugs, whereafter they re-joined the jeeps for the rest of their tour. As it was after noon, and heading for the hottest part of the day, the insects were out in force, and as soon as the jeeps returned beneath the canopy of trees, its occupants were attacked and bitten mercilessly.

It was Wuffles whose phobia of all insects finally broke her. 'I can't stand this anymore,' she shouted, waving her hands around in the air to disperse a cloud of little flying beasties that had surrounded her for a feast. 'I can practically see their bibs and cruet sets.' As this cry rang out, there was a chorus of screams from many of the others in the jeeps, as Horseface pointed out the long cylindrical body of a snake that was dangling from a tree under which they had just passed.

'Stop!' shouted Windy, managing to make herself heard by both jeep drivers – she really had retained a stentorian voice since her schooldays – and advised both men that there was a problem. 'What do you want to do?' she asked in general, but of Wuffles in particular.

'I want to go back to where the ferry docked. At least there was a breeze there, and it kept the insects away. I can't stand this any longer.'

'And the snake,' came a call from the other jeep.

'Let's go back, Windy.' There was a general chorus of agreement between all of them and the drivers took the quickest route to the shoreline. They were at least an hour ahead of time, but they may prove to be lucky.

They were, and Goodluck Johnston hadn't gone off about other business, but had stayed put, talking to other boat users and old friends, thoroughly enjoying his day off. Not only had he got to go visiting, but he had made money as well, and good money, from this group of rich old pussies. He also had high hopes of the forecast storm developing, and getting a few days just chilling, while the seas were too rough for him to operate the ferry.

The stiff breeze they had left behind them on arrival was now a rising wind, and little white caps were developing on the waves of the channel between the islands. It was, after all, the Atlantic out there, and things could get pretty rough in no time at all. Windy gave it as her opinion that it had been a wise move to leave early as, if they'd waited any longer, it might have been too rough for them to get back home.

Her mind, on the return journey, was totally consumed with what had to be taken in from the garden, and what other storm precautions were to be instituted and replicated by all the girls, when Horseface asked her if the island they had just visited was the one they would fly back from. 'Not at all. It doesn't even have a landing strip for small planes,' Windy informed her distractedly. 'The planes go from the bigger island to the north.'

'And how will we get there when we go?' asked Horseface earnestly. 'Is it the same ferry?'

'No, you need to go from the north ferry landing stage, the other side of the cruise terminal,' she finished, and flapped her hands at the other woman to get back into the train of thought that she had reluctantly been brought out of to answer irrelevant questions.

The wind continued to rise, and the ferry not only bobbed up and down, but rocked sideways as well in a movement that the ferryman described as 'corkscrewing', and after which Lady

Amanda thought she might need to use one of those herself, for she felt like she would deserve a large drink after all this tossing and turning in nothing more substantial than a large old bathtub. It hadn't been a very pleasant day, so far.

At least one old girl had been ill over the side of the ferry on the way over; the jeep trip had been a nightmare on those rutted roads, and she felt very bruised and battered; lunch had been a poorly-cooked fiasco, and the attack of the ravenous insects had been horrible too, she thought as she scratched vigorously at a little nest of bites on her right shoulder. And that snake had just been the end. If Wuffles hadn't suddenly cracked, she feared it would have been she, Lady Amanda Golightly, who showed cowardice in the face of the enemy.

Hugo, who was sitting vigorously scratching at both his knees, looked up and commented, 'Been a rum old day, hasn't it? I, for one, shall be glad to get back, won't you?'

'I will that, Hugo. Large glass of something relaxing when we get in,' she replied, now applying the sharpness of her fingernails to her ankles. 'I seem to have been bitten to bits.'

When they had docked and sent a runner to locate Winstone Churchill, Windy suggested that they go back to their own properties, and make preparations for the approaching storm. 'All rubbish bins are to be put in the exterior storage cupboards, all windows and doors are to be closed and locked, and also all shutters to be fastened tightly. Anything that might be blown away by a strong wind has to be either brought indoors or stored. Any questions?'

'Are the villas built to withstand the storms you get out here?' asked a nervous Fflageolet.

'Silly girl! Of course they are, otherwise they wouldn't have withstood the first winter. We made sure they were built to the correct standard necessary not to blow down at the first hint of a tropical storm, and this probably won't be a full tropical one, just a precursor of what's to come later in the year. It's a bit early, yet, for the stormy weather to set in. This will give you a demonstration that I couldn't possibly have arranged for you, to see just how sturdy the structures are.'

By now, several of the old girls were on their knees, heads over the side of the ferry, and Windy was sure that most of what had been said hadn't been taken in, so she'd make sure she repeated her instructions on the bus, when most of her old school chums weren't too busy throwing up their goat or chicken stew over the side, to provide sustenance for the local fish.

Thus reassured, their trip home in the old wreck of a bus was in virtual silence, apart from Windy's reiteration of the necessary storm preparations, and they left the vehicle in a very subdued manner, each heading for their own villa. As they disembarked from the bus, Wuffles muttered in Lady A's ear, 'You will keep me under your hat, won't you? I don't want my cover broken.'

There had been a tacit agreement between Lady Amanda and Beauchamp that, when the newly-weds had secured their property, if there was no danger to life or limb, they would go across to number fifteen, and have cocktails together. She had not yet had a chance to inform them of what she had learnt about Wuffles' true reasons for being on the island, and another couple of pairs of eyes might make all the difference. It wouldn't be an issue telling those two, although she wouldn't let on to any of the others, not even Windy.

Chapter Thirteen

Back in number fifteen, Lady A and Hugo were enjoying a very large glass of chilled white wine. It was Manda who had had to wield the corkscrew, Hugo's hands being too arthritic to allow the necessary gripping and pulling power. After a hearty swallow, he turned to his companion and said, 'Gracious, Manda, if I ever stopped living with you, I'd have to start buying wine in screw-top bottles, or I'd never get a quiet drink, for I couldn't stand having to go to a bar just for a glass of wine.'

'Don't be a silly billy, Hugo. The only reason you wouldn't be living with me would be if either you or I were dead. If something happened to you, you wouldn't have the need to open wine anymore, and if something happened to me, I've put it in my will that you are to live out the remainder of your days in Belchester Towers, when it would then revert to Beauchamp, so if I'm gone, you'll always have him there to deal with bottles of wine, port or difficult cans and jars.'

Hugo wiped a tear from his eye, not sure

whether he was moved by the thought that one or other of them must die first, or by Manda's very generous alteration to her will, so that he need never go back into a home again. He was soon snapped out of this uncharacteristically sentimental mood, however, by a furious knocking on the front door. Whoever could that be, with the wind now starting to howl, and the first of the rain beginning to fall? It surely couldn't be Beauchamp and Enid, who would certainly never consider making an uncivilised racket like that.

The staff helping out in the villas had been dismissed and allowed to go home to secure their own properties, and Lady Amanda thus rose to answer this urgent summons. On the doorstep, she found Windy, her hair and kaftan blowing all over the place, an envelope which she could barely hold onto clutched in her hand.

'Come in! Come on in out of that ghastly weather and tell me whatever's the matter with you, Windy, old girl.' Lady A stood aside to admit her visitor, and pushed against the wind to close the door again. 'What is it?' she asked again, surveying the bedraggled, windswept wreck that was her next door neighbour.

'We've had another one of those letters,' she gasped, her breath quite taken away by the force of the wind, as she held out the hand still clutching the envelope for Lady A's inspection.

'The weather's certainly living up to your nickname, isn't it?' the recipient of this damp missive asked rhetorically, then the words on the piece of paper that she had extracted from the envelope silenced her completely. When she had recovered

172

from her shock, she asked, 'When did this come?'

'I've no idea,' replied Windy. 'It could have been put in the mailbox anytime from yesterday evening onwards, as we didn't bother checking the box this morning, and I found it when I was going about storm protection measures. We daren't risk there being anything left in there in case the mailbox is uprooted and blown away.'

'"Two hundred and fifty thousand pounds in cash buys my silence,"' read Lady Amanda, in awe of the size of the sum and the audacity of the sender. '"I will be in touch about time and place." How on earth are you going to deal with this?'

'I haven't the faintest idea. All the money's gone on maintaining the properties, and after the global crash of the housing market and all that, we didn't get what we'd hoped for them.' Windy was very good at manipulating the truth. 'If we don't sell a couple more, we won't even be able to live here, let alone further the development of the site.'

Lady Amanda knew better than this, having had that little snoop in Cocktails, while all the others were doing the viewing rounds, but kept her silence. She realised that she knew what the black-mailer knew, and she had, so far, not said a word to Hugo, or Beauchamp and Enid. She made a quick decision that she should leave things as they were, and decided that a bit of carefully worded enquiry of the other old girls might elicit the fact that one of them knew more than she ought to.

'Let's show this to Hugo,' she said, leading her neighbour into the sitting room, but had to leave Hugo with the letter in his hands, as there was a more discreet knock on the door, and she opened it to find Enid and Beauchamp, an optimistic but nevertheless inside-out umbrella in the former's hand. She had to get the butler to close the door, as the force of the storm was really too great for her now, and she led them into the sitting room where she had left the other two.

'I say, this is a bit rich isn't it?' asked Hugo, waving around the sheet of paper with its gummed on message. 'How on earth do you get hold of such a large amount of cash on a small island like this, in a hurry?'

'That's just it,' replied Windy with great anxiety. 'Not only is it impossible to get hold of a huge sum like that without a great deal of fuss and intrusive paperwork, but we simply don't have that sort of money.' Beauchamp took the sheet of paper from Hugo, and he and Enid read it.

'How ghastly!' exclaimed Enid. 'And you've absolutely no idea who sent this?'

'None whatsoever.'

At this point, Lady Amanda decided that it would be a good idea to rid themselves of Windy's company, so that they could have a good old natter about developments about which two of them knew nothing, and something else she hadn't mentioned, about which none of them knew.

'I'll just get these two a glass of wine before they fight their way back, and I really think you ought to be going, too, Windy. The weather's not getting any calmer, and at least Enid has Beauchamp's muscle-power to help her get home. I think you ought to get back to Beep-Beep. He must be worried sick about the storm.'

'I just hope he's back,' she replied.

174

'Back from where?' was asked in chorus.

'From securing all the empty villas from storm damage. They were all open for you lot to look round. If he leaves them with windows unlocked, and with the shutters open, they could be wrecked. It's the wind breaching the barrier between inside and out that does the real damage.'

A strong sense of guilt pervaded the other three in the room, totally uncalled for, because they could not have foreseen the sudden change in the weather, but this was alleviated by a couple of stout thumps on the front door, and Beauchamp went to answer it only to find Beep-Beep standing there, looking like the wreck of the *Hesperus*.

'Are you finished already?' asked Beauchamp, admitting and, with some difficulty, shutting out the storm.

'I left Windy shutting up our place, and started immediately; then, when I got back just now, I found a note from her saying she'd come round here to show you the letter. I'll take her back home, now, so that we can ride out the storm together. You see if you can come up with any ideas as to who the blackmailer could be.'

Windy, hearing his voice in the hall, rushed out, and the two of them went back into the dark and stormy night mentioned in so many gothic horror stories. 'I know why they're so worried,' stated Lady A out of the blue. 'And I think I know who the blackmailer is, as well.'

'You do?'

'Who is it?'

'How did you find out?'

Their hostess smiled, and began to give them the

lowdown. 'When I was on my little viewing trip the other day, I hung behind especially so that I could go through the pedal bins and waste-paper baskets inside the houses. I'd already gone through the outside bins when you were all partying.'

'Good grief! You never said anything,' Beauchamp interrupted with some surprise. He thought he and Enid were in on everything the woman did.

'There hasn't been much time to talk to either of you since we left dear old Belchester Towers,' stated his employer baldly. 'Anyway, on my trip through the gardens while you were all drinking cocktails, I discovered evidence of a small fire in the garden of number seven. When I went through the pedal bin while I should have been avidly viewing the properties, I found some slips of paper which I suspected found their way in there more by accident than design.

'I suspect that whoever sent the letters gathered together what she thought of as all her "snippings", then burned them out at the back. If she missed any perhaps one of the others found them on the floor and slipped them into the nearest waste-paper basket without another thought about them.'

'Who's staying in that villa?' asked Hugo, now all ears.

'Wuffles, Droopy-Drawers, and Longshanks,' she answered.

'Well, we can discount Wuffles because...'

'Shut up, Hugo,' barked Lady A. Hugo shut up like a clam. 'It's only because he's taken a liking to her – reminds him of an old dog he had as a boy. Take no notice. Now, I have something else I discovered that I haven't told you yet.'

Hugo looked pained. Manda had said nothing about the piece of Customs and Excise paper, nor the 'meet me at midnight' note, nor his eavesdropping from the other night. What was she up to? But he daren't ask her before their guests had left. It was evidently something that she wanted to keep to herself.

Lady Amanda had her own agenda, though, and wanted to keep information in its correct pigeon-holes: first, any information concerning the blackmail, then a *précis* about what they had learnt about Wuffles. 'Going back to it being one of those three women, I have evidence, as well, of why Windy and Beep-Beep are so unwilling to share this information with the authorities, or with any of the other old girls.' At this, Hugo looked up in surprise. Whatever else had she found? A few bits of paper were one thing, but this sounded far more important.

'While I was in Cocktails yesterday, on my riffle through pedal bins and suchlike, I happened to take a good look in Beep-Beep's desk. I found bank statements that show that a very large amount of money has passed through their account, but has almost completely been spent – or moved.'

There were gasps of surprise at this. 'Windy wasn't kidding,' she went on, 'when she said they didn't have much money in their island account, and certainly not enough to pay off a blackmailer. But there seems to have been another account, although I couldn't really decipher very much, as it was in another language. She was only telling a half-truth. I think a lot of money's been transferred to an account that no one but them – and now we – know about.

'I also discovered a lease in there, too. If I tell you what was in it, you must promise not to indicate by word, look or deed, what I am about to tell you.' There were actions of crossing hearts and cutting throats as the other three present stood in silence, wondering what on earth she was going to come out with next.

'It was a lease for the land that Parrot Bay is built on. It was from the owner of the island, and specified no other land to be developed later. It also specified a period of only fifteen years for the lease, and it was signed ten years ago. No wonder those two are so eager to sell the other properties – so that they could make a run for it and follow their money.' This information was greeted with complete silence, the shock at the duplicity of such an outwardly nice couple, being as hard to digest as a lead sandwich.

'The reason I believe there were such large sums paid out of their bank account, is because I have the sneaking suspicion that they've been moving it to an account in South America – the language in which the letter I noticed seemed to be Spanish – where they've no doubt set up new identities, and established a base to which they can flee. These anonymous letters have put a spanner in their works big-time.'

This was such a dreadful revelation that Wuffles was not mentioned again, and Beauchamp and Enid left shortly afterwards, without anything else having been disclosed to them.

Hugo sat absolutely immobile on a sofa, dumb-founded and as silent as a ventriloquist's dummy lacking the ventriloquist to pull his levers. 'I thought,' began Lady Amanda, 'it was best not to get involved with telling them about what Wuffles is up to. There seems to be a much more serious situation involving the embezzlement of funds, and fraudulent leases issued to her old school chums. I simply don't know what to do about it. Have you got any ideas?'

Hugo sat on in silence. The evening seemed to have passed very quickly, and he needed time to think about how he could disguise his knowledge of Windy and Beep-Beep's criminal behaviour, and not let this show when he met them again. He was a naturally honest man, and he had a feeling that everything would be visible in his face when-ever he had to speak to them. In that case, he'd better do his best to avoid them, no matter how inconvenient this proved, although Manda had managed to give nothing away about what she had discovered when they came round earlier.

After an hour or so, during which Hugo still had not said anything, he announced that he thought he'd go up to bed, and left the room with the more comfortable gait that he had adopted in the higher temperatures of this island paradise. But there had been a snake in Eden. And he knew now that there were at least two snakes on Caribbaya, and he had no inclination to tangle with either of them, ever again.

Lady Amanda had taken her discoveries more in her stride, but she sat on, thinking how on earth she could seek justice for her old chums who had purchased properties on the island. After about forty-five minutes, she decided to go out for a walk, as the wind had dropped considerably; maybe the storm had veered off somewhere else. A brisk walk along the beach would do her thought processes the world of good, and the wind would help to blow away the cobwebs in her mind.

It was still gusty outside, but bearable, and she headed straight for the sand of the beach, where she could look out to sea. The sky had cleared a little, and there was some starlight. Looking up in the darkness always made her feel calm, and allayed any fears she had about everyday life. She was so small and insignificant in comparison to the vastness of space that she completely relaxed and it always helped her to clear her mind, or make it up about something that had been bothering her.

She did this at Belchester Towers, too, looking up and to the north, so that her view should not be detracted from by the orange glow that showed above the small city. To the north was open countryside for some miles. She usually slipped out of a back door so that no one knew what she was up to, but she had the feeling that Beauchamp suspected, as she was always so much more placid and decisive the next day.

She made the decision that it would all have to come out, and that she would have to get together all those who had bought properties, and persuade them to get in touch with the owner of the island, explain how they had been duped, and see if he would issue a ninety-nine year lease, or something close to it, so that they did not lose their investment completely. There didn't seem to be any other solution.

She would have to have a word with that police inspector if he ever came back to the island, or go to the security service that passed for police, based near the jewellery quarter. Beauchamp would know how to go about things: she'd have to consult him.

Turning to make her way back to number fifteen, she saw, once again, that tall figure, disappearing down the beach but, when she turned her head slightly, she saw another figure disappear behind the villas. Who the hell was that? Grabbing her kaftan to make running – or the best attempt she could make at it – easier, she was off. When she got to the back of the properties, however, there was no one in sight, and there were no lights on in any of the villas. She could hardly knock everybody up and ask them if somebody had just had a clandestine meeting with someone else, possibly a smuggler, could she? It might have been a date, for all she knew.

All the evidence, so far, pointed at that person being in Wuffles' house, but she had no desire to call there and risk blowing the Customs investigator's cover. This was something else to keep to herself for now. She knew that walk that the first figure had had, however. She had seen it several times now, but just couldn't nail down who it was.

It was like looking through a distorting mirror, where you have difficulty in recognising your own face. At the moment, she hadn't connected the conversation that Hugo had overheard as being anything other than a clandestine meeting of would-be lovers.

Anyway, the wind was getting up again, and the cloud cover was returning, so she'd certainly better get back before the light went completely behind cloud cover, or the electricity went off. Or worse.

At a house across the close, a figure had just slipped into the back garden and into the house as silently as possible. It then mounted the stairs without putting on any lights and went into the spare room where it had concealed its night-clothes. A quick change, and the figure was ready to slip into its room, knowing that it was going to get away with this part of the plan, but with severe misgivings about the next part.

The figure did, indeed, get into bed without rousing anyone, even managing to slip the clothes worn that evening into the chest of drawers. But sleep didn't come easily, and half the night passed before this blessed escape was achieved. Thus, the severance of the electricity supply was noticed by no one in Parrot Bay until the next morning.

Lady Amanda also lay awake for some time, mulling over what she had seen on her little stroll. The plot was definitely thickening. She just wished she'd had some excuse – any old excuse – for making such a late-night call on number seven, but even if she could have thought up a plausible reason for the visit, she didn't want to panic Wuffles. She'd have to speak to her tomorrow about her experiences on the beach.

Chapter Fourteen

As the residents awoke the next morning, the first thing everyone did was look out of their bedroom window. The storm had calmed a little, but it had had its fun with the island, vegetation uprooted or torn from its plant was strewn everywhere, and any grass that had grown just a couple of inches was flattened by the fierceness of the overnight wind.

As the girls got dressed, they all decided that there would have to be a grand clear-up, and made their way outside to establish a working party. They had gathered together a great pile of branches and palm fronds when Winstone Churchill drew into the road in his taxi, with a fanfare of greeting on his horn. Whoever could this be?

Lady Amanda and Windy approached it as the man got out and opened the door for his passenger, disgorging a very forlorn-looking Horseface on to the narrow sidewalk, a heavily laden rucksack on her back.

'What on earth are you doing out of the close at this hour?' asked Windy. 'Where have you been?'

Without a word, Horseface strode off towards number one without a reply, and it was left to Winstone to provide them with information. 'Ah found her down at de north dock, blown every which way an' soaked to de skin. She said she'd walked down from Parrot Bay – in *dis* weather. I tole her she must be mad, but she said she was waitin' for de ferry to get to de north island to get a plane home. I said there was no way she was gettin' off Caribbaya for at least a couple of days, with de storm not blown out and liable to come back, and she really lost her rag wid me.

'I tole her, it wasn't mah fault, and that she wouldn't have been able to get a flight today anyway, as there would only have been a flight to de mainland today, and not a transatlantic one. If she wanted an on-going flight, it would have been tomorrow, but all dat's dependent on de wedder. Den she burst into tears and begged me to find a way for her to get away.

'Well, dere weren't nothin' Ah could do, so I brought her back here, but she sure is in a black mood, and Ah don' know why. Wot she want to leave here early for, anyway? And why she got no proper suitcase? She must-a left half her stuff behind in de house.'

'Thank you very much for taking care of her and bringing her back here,' said Windy appreciatively. 'If the wind comes back, anything could have happened to her. I'll go down there now. Are you coming, Sniffy?'

'Too right, I am,' said Lady A, scenting that the hunt was on.

Fflageolet had seen the arrival of her housemate, and hurried over to number one to see what was going on and where Horseface had been. She'd not checked her room when she got up, just assuming that the other woman was still asleep and would join them when she woke.

184

She was first through the door, and found Horseface sitting on the sofa, curled into a ball and sobbing her heart out. 'Whatever's happened to get you in a state like this?' she asked, sitting beside the bedraggled and desolate figure and putting an arm around her shoulders.

'Nothing. Leave me alone,' was the only reply. Fflageolet handed her a tissue from the box on the coffee table so that she could blow her nose, as there were twin trickles of mucous decorating her face when she looked up briefly – what Matron at school had referred to as a 'number eleven' on the top lip.

Before either of them had the chance to say anything else, Lady Amanda and Windy burst in through the door and asked what the hell was going on. 'Why did you just go like that?' asked Windy. 'Did someone here upset you so much that you felt you had to run away?'

'I wasn't rudding away,' replied Horseface, her blocked nose distorting her speech. 'I just wadded to go home.'

'But you're not a quitter – or at least, you never used to be. Whatever has happened for you to react like this?'

'It's nothig. Just be being ibbature.'

'But you were a bit jumpy yesterday, so something's obviously happened that's unsettled you,' Lady A commented.

At this, Horseface launched herself from the sofa and hurtled out of the room, where they heard her furious stamping upstairs, and the slam of her bedroom door.

'I can't think what's got her into such a state,'

said Fflageolet. 'If you just leave her here, maybe I can get something out of her when she calms down.'

'*If* she calms down,' commented Windy with an indignant sniff. She had never been walked out on like this before, not even at school. Her power had been absolute, and she always got her own way. Until now.

'Come on, let's get back outside,' suggested Lady A. She really didn't want to be cooped up with Windy any longer than was decently necessary. She needed time to think what she was going to do about what she knew about the ownership – or not – of the houses that had, seemingly, been lawfully purchased. She needed to consult with Hugo. She also needed to talk to Beauchamp and Enid; four heads were better than two.

When the old girls had finished clearing up as best as they could, they went back to their various bases, the storm being expected to return, only with greater force than the night before. It simply wasn't worth it trying to go anywhere or do anything. Inside was best, with the shutters tightly fastened, and the lights on.

As they dispersed, Lady Amanda indicated to Beauchamp that she and Hugo would be going back to their place. It was better if they weren't quite so handy for Windy to drop in on them. Hugo was a little confused when she steered him towards number eight, but he soon caught on that there was to be a putting together of heads. Something had to be done before any of the other girls tried to buy one of the villas on the close. He didn't know what they could do about those old

186

girls who had already lashed out large sums, but they could certainly put a halt to any other sales.

Number eight was of a much more open-plan design than number fifteen, the downstairs comprising one big area which encompassed the living area, a dining space, and a zoned kitchen. It must have got an incredible amount of light when the shutters weren't closed.

'This is much nicer than ours, with the three different rooms,' said Hugo, looking around with pleasure.

'Yes, but it doesn't have the same floor space as our three rooms combined,' replied Lady Amanda, slightly put out that the honeymooners had been allocated this American-style villa. She'd have been very happy with it herself.

'Not so good for permanent living, though,' Enid consoled her. 'Entertaining would be a nightmare, with all the pots and pans on display while you tried to conduct a civilised dinner party. And you're hardly likely to be purchasing one anyway, given what you told us last night.'

'How do we go about resolving the matter though? That's the knotty question.' Lady Amanda looked hopefully at Beauchamp, whom she had previously considered to be the fount of all knowledge. 'What can we do, Beauchamp?'

'The first thing we need to do is to find out if anyone's approached her with an interest in buying. If they have, we have to warn them that they mustn't part with any money,' he said, most sensibly.

'But how do we do that without raising suspicion, or alerting Windy and Beep-Beep?' Lady

Amanda's concern could be heard in her voice. She didn't want all those old friends to lose their life-savings in a wicked scam like this, perpetrated by their former head girl.

'I don't think that can be avoided. We've got to rat on them at some point, and they'll probably make a run for it, once they've got wind of what we know, but that can't be helped,' he continued. 'I don't think we can avoid raising suspicion, but that would stop them getting their hands on any more money. What we can do for those that have already been fleeced is a bit more difficult. We'll have to come up with a pretty nifty scheme to stop them losing out completely. Leave it with me, and I'll see what I can come up with.'

'As you're here, do you want to stay to lunch?' asked Enid, now the considerate hostess. 'I could rustle us up something pretty quickly, if you'd like to stay.'

Hugo agreed enthusiastically, Lady Amanda merely nodding, lost in thought. After a while, she said, 'I suppose I could go round to Windy's and ask her if there had been any interest in the villas after our mass viewing, when we get back. I've been keeping a straight face and a zipped lip so far.'

'That's a jolly good idea, Manda. Just don't ask me to go with you. I don't think I could look either of them in the eye again.'

'I wouldn't trust you not to say something,' came the slightly derogatory reply, but she wasn't really paying attention, her thoughts running ahead of her actions, concerning the proposed invasion of what she now saw as enemy territory.

In just under half an hour, Enid served up ham, salad, and mashed sweet potatoes, a combination that was acceptable to all four of them, with a fruit salad for dessert, then coffee, taken back on the softer upholstery of the twin sofas. Lady Amanda still held her peace about the possibility of smugglers – apart from Adonis and his emeralds – and when the clock struck three, she suggested to Hugo that they really ought to get back to number fifteen.

'Do we have to?' he asked, with his lower lip stuck out petulantly, making Enid laugh at his resemblance to a mutinous schoolboy.

'Yes we do, but don't worry; you won't have to see either of them. I'll go round and sweet-talk her then, when I leave, I'll say we've already got plans for the evening. I'll say we're coming here, if I may, so that, if necessary, we can grab the keys and look ready to go out if she does chance her arm and come round.'

'That's fine by me,' answered Enid, before Beauchamp had the chance to get a word in. She was certainly mistress of this house, although that would of course not be the case when they got back to Belchester Towers. 'I can always rustle up a quiche or something if you do need to flee here.'

'You are a kind soul, Enid,' Hugo thanked her, leaving Beauchamp with his mouth open, not having managed to get a word in, of agreement or otherwise.

Back in their own space, Hugo started to look anxious and furtive. 'Are you going, then?' he asked, almost as soon as he had closed the front door, having allowed Manda to precede him, as good manners dictated.

'Give me a moment, old thing. I've got to get my mind round looking completely innocent, and pleased if she's got anyone else on the hook. I need to arrange my thoughts so that I'm in the right frame of mind.'

'Well, get a move on, then. I don't want her turning up round here. I just can't face her again.'

'Look, if she comes to the door, you can get yourself off upstairs, and I'll say you've gone to bed with a sick headache, due to being out in the wind this morning. I'm going to have a quick vodka and tonic, for Dutch courage. I'll only be a few minutes, while I wait for it to take effect.'

'I'll be in my room until you go.' Hugo's courage had failed him, and he couldn't stand the suspense of the woman maybe turning up at any moment.

'Coward!' called Lady A, after his retreating figure, as she drained her glass and waited for the alcohol to hit her brain.

As the muscles in her shoulders got the message and relaxed, she threw down a refill just to help, then set off determinedly towards Cocktails, a smile plastered all over her face. Two large vodkas, and this spy stuff was easy-peasy – as long as the alcohol didn't loosen her tongue and allow her to let out something she hadn't meant to. Pulling herself together, she rang the doorbell, and knocked as well, as the wind was getting up again.

'Hello there, Sniffy. What can I do for you?' Windy greeted her, holding on to the door so that it wasn't snatched out of her hand.

'Just seeking a bit of sanctuary,' she shouted above the howling that had just begun. 'Hugo's gone to bed with a sick headache, and I fancied a bit of company.'

Poor thing – Hugs, that is. Come on in. I've got some rather exciting news, anyway, so I was just going to pop round to you.' So Hugo had been right. If Lady A hadn't left when she did, Windy would have been at their door.

'What weather,' exclaimed the visitor, 'just like you, really: Windy by name and windy by nature.' She suddenly shut up, realising that it was that second vodka speaking for her. 'May I come in?'

'Yes, do. Can I get you a cocktail or something?'

'I'd prefer tea, if you don't mind, but you go ahead and have a cocktail. I'll raise my cup to you as if I were having one too.'

'You're on,' replied Windy, rushing to put on the kettle before she got busy making herself a martini. That was good. Lady Amanda could let her drink it and just keep to small talk, while the martini was getting into her bloodstream, and the vodka was working its way out of *her* pores.

Having served them both, Windy held up her glass and said, 'Bottoms up,' while Lady A raised her teacup, repeating the salutation. 'I've got some fab news,' she continued, only to be interrupted by, 'Oh, but I must tell you about this lunchtime – before Hugo got his headache,' which she'd just remembered in time. 'Your news will keep a few minutes, I'm sure. We went over to number eight; you know, where the Beauchamps are having their honeymoon...' She wrung every little detail she could out of the rather uneventful luncheon, even

191

including the invitation, which wasn't quite as she told it, to dinner tonight, but that would only happen if Hugo was feeling better.

'Did he take something for it?' asked Windy.

'For what?' That vodka must have been taken in double measures.

'For his headache, silly.'

'Sorry. It must be the wind that's distracting me. Now, where was I?'

'I rather think it's my turn now. Listen to this. After the mass viewings, both Droopy-Drawers and Fflageolet have approached me about buying the villas they're staying in. Obviously they won't be able to give us a deposit at the moment, because all communications with the island are down, and both want to speak to their bank managers first, just to confirm that it's alright to take such a large sum out of the country, but this is really good news for me and Beep-Beep.'

Lady Amanda swallowed hard. Things were further advanced than she'd hoped, but they'd have to do something before the island got its communications back. Those two old girls were just ripe for being persuaded that they could transfer the money for the deposit without consultation with their financial advisors, and she wasn't letting these two fraudsters get away with any more money than they had done already.

'Knowing the shambles they can make with communications on the island, it'll probably be a couple of days before anything's up and running again, but that's not too much time. We can wait.' The last three words were uttered with little conviction, and Lady A's mind began to swirl with a seething mass of thoughts.

She, Hugo, and the Beauchamps were going to have to talk to those two would-be investors and warn them off. If they blew the gaff, then so be it, but she couldn't permit them to put down a deposit on villas on a plot of land that had such a short lease. If the four of them got together and talked it through, they might be able to get the old girls to wait a bit, so that they could alert the authorities to what Windy and Beep-Beep had been up to, and maybe even get them arrested.

That still left the problem of the monies already paid, but that would have to wait till later. They could only solve one crime at a time, and passing on what they knew would be future crime prevention. And they'd have to persuade those who were proposing to purchase not to let on to the others who already had. Blast! Life could be really thorny at times.

'Would you like to come here for supper instead of fighting your way over to number eight?' asked Windy, who was feeling rather sociable, what with her good news, and the effects of the rather vermouth-free martini she had just imbibed.

'Oh don't worry about us; we'll be fine. If Hugo's not feeling up to going to the Beauchamps', I shall have an early night, and if he is, we're both of us far too heavy to get blown away.'

'You'd be surprised at how strong the wind can get here,' Windy countered.

'We'll be fine. Don't worry. It's been a busy few days, and if we can't get out, it would be nice just to relax a bit and have an early night. You have kept us to a pretty tight schedule since we got here,' said Lady Amanda, looking entirely innocent.

'I needed to get you all to fall in love with the island in general, and with the villas in particular, so I wanted to keep you as busy as possible and not have any annoying bridge parties, or have you get up to any other antics that didn't involve Caribbaya and Parrot Bay's lovely homes.'

'Well, thanks for the tea. I'd better be getting back now, to see if Hugo is awake enough to handle a cup of tea.'

'If you must.'

Lady Amanda left Cocktails with a feeling of great relief washing over her. She had managed to extract the information she wanted, and had managed not to let anything slip about what was known about the background of embezzlement: but she definitely shouldn't have had that second vodka and tonic.

After her return, she and Hugo managed quite a good scratch tea between them, just using bits and pieces left in the fridge and the larder, and were sitting digesting this when there was a furious knocking on the door, barely audible what with the noise of the wind and the lashing rain.

Hurriedly ushering in Fflageolet, Lady Amanda noticed the woman's concerned face, which was deathly pale, and asked her whatever the matter was. 'It's Horseface: she seems to be in dreadful pain, and she won't tell me what's wrong. I simply don't know what to do with her. She's just curled up on her bed holding her stomach and groaning with pain, muttering, "No, no, no, not now, not yet." You don't think she could be pregnant, do you?'

'That's hardly likely, given her advanced years, is it?' barked Lady Amanda, sounding unsympathetic in her worry. 'We'll come back with you, but go and pick up Beauchamp on the way. He's done a first aid course, and he might be able to work out what's wrong with her, or what might help with the pain. Ignore that. I'll collect Beauchamp. You're of such a slight build I'm surprised you didn't get blown away on your trip over here. Just hang on to Hugo. He'll make a pretty effective anchor.'

'Thanks,' muttered Hugo under his breath. 'So that's what I am now, is it, an anchor for light old ladies?'

'Come along, old chap. Pay attention, and escort this lady back home. Number one, isn't it?' she asked Fflageolet, who nodded in agreement.

Without another word, Lady Amanda let herself out, pushing the door closed as Hugo fumbled for his jacket – as if that would do anything to protect him in this maelstrom – and shambled as quickly as she could across to number eight to alert Beauchamp that they had a medical emergency on their hands.

Fflageolet and Hugo found the situation to be just as Fflageolet had described, with Horseface writhing in pain on her bed, still moaning in denial of something. 'What is it, old girl?' asked Hugo taking what he considered the considerable liberty of sitting on the edge of her mattress. 'What has made you so ill?'

'What was in that dish you made at lunchtime,' she managed to gasp out.

'It was just a bit of tomato sauce with garlic and pasta,' replied Fflageolet.

'It was more than that. Think!'

'I put in a dollop of the local hot sauce, as there was a bottle of it in the larder. I didn't want it to go off.'

Horseface gasped, then gave a loud hollow moan and clutched at her middle. 'You stupid fool! You've no idea what you've done, have you?'

'What are you talking about?'

A chorus of yells interrupted this interesting but uninformative conversation, announcing the arrival of not just Lady Amanda and Beauchamp, but of Enid as well. She had insisted on coming with them, as she'd had all those years of experience looking after her mother: and also in case it was anything delicate that Horseface didn't want disclosed to her old school friends.

Having been admitted to the house by Fflageolet, they went upstairs to join the throng, only to have Beauchamp take in the seriousness of Horseface's plight, and send her housemate, Lady Amanda, and Hugo downstairs, so that he and Enid could try to find out exactly what had got her into this situation.

They left a little grumpily at not being involved in the action, but appreciated that there was not room in the bedroom for them all. Fflageolet allayed her fears with the distraction of making tea, while Hugo sat patiently, Lady A impatiently on a sofa to await any news.

Back in the bedroom, Enid sat down on the edge of the bed, held Horseface's hand, and asked her what had caused this parlous state of affairs. 'Can't tell you,' she wailed, clutching at her middle again, then whimpering, 'Oh no, oh no, not now. Please God, not now.'

'What seems to be the problem?' asked Enid in a soft, concerned voice.

Beauchamp sat on the other side of the bed and took the woman's other hand, now not wrapped round her middle. 'Is it something you've eaten?' he asked.

Pulling both hands down to the lower end of her abdomen, she cried out in anguish, and grunted, 'Yes. Hot sauce.'

'Then, you're probably just in for a bout of the runs, like Hugo had. Let's get you to the bathroom,' advised Enid.

'I can't! I can't! Not on the lavatory. I just can't,' Horseface cried out, clutching once more at the lower end of her body.

'Why not?' asked Beauchamp.

'He'll kill me for sure. And if he doesn't, someone else from above will,' was grunted at him.

'Whatever are you talking about? Who will kill you? And what's this about someone from above?' asked the butler, in a reassuring voice.

'Get her to get a bucket,' Horseface enunciated with difficulty. 'I'll tell you, but I don't want anyone else to know: only you,' she informed Beauchamp.

'Do as she says,' he said, turning round to look at Enid, 'and when you get back, hand it through to me, then join the others downstairs.' Enid did as she had been instructed. It would seem that her husband had won the poor patient's confidence, and she had to talk to someone. Whatever had she done to herself?

When she got back downstairs and sat down beside Hugo, Fflageolet asked, 'Is she being sick now? At least it'll get whatever's upset her out of her system.'

'I've no idea what's going on up there. I was definitely persona non-grata, but we can leave it to Beechy. She'll confide in him. He has that sort of effect on people, getting them to tell him their troubles.'

Lady Amanda winced as she heard this abominable diminutive of her butler's name, but realised that things were out of her hands now. As far as Beauchamp was concerned, she only had domestic power over him. It was Enid who would be the mainstay of his life, now they were married.

In the bedroom, Horseface was very slowly giving up her tale of woe and the perilous situation in which she was going to find herself. Beauchamp's first question when Enid discreetly handed the bucket round the door was, 'Do you want to be sick?'

'No,' came the reply, filled with pain.

'What do you want to do, then?'

'Can't tell you.'

'1 think you realise that you have to. If you're in any danger, you need as many people fighting for your corner as you can get,' he warned her.

Slowly, her tale of troubles began to unravel, in between waves of pain.

Horseface had been a probation officer in her working life, and had recently been sought out by one of her ex-regular 'clients', a fearsome gangster that she'd been in such terror of that she'd eventually handed his case on to one of her colleagues. He had always been involved in drug distribution, and he told her that he wanted her to do a 'little job' for him.

Somehow, he had heard about her upcoming trip to Caribbaya, and he had been given the name of a contact on the island. Knowing that she'd always feared him, he'd informed her that she was wanted as a drugs mule, being of a perfect age to avoid suspicion, and that if she didn't comply, then he'd make sure that drugs were found in her home, following an anonymous tip-off to the police. That would really mess up the last quarter of her life, and she would lose any respect she had enjoyed from her family and friends, he'd sneered.

When that didn't quite work, he'd simply threatened to cut her face off.

That had been enough to convince Horseface to come over here and make the required contact with the person next up the chain. At the moment, she wasn't willing to divulge who that was, but what she did tell Beauchamp was that she had been persuaded to swallow a number of condoms stuffed with heroin.

Not only had she been foolish enough to ingest them before she went to bed for a few hours' sleep the night before, but then she had honestly believed she could get a ferry to the north island the next morning, and pick up a direct flight back to England. Then Fflageolet, in her innocence, had spiced up their lunch with a liberal helping of hot sauce.

At this point, the pain became much worse, and

Beauchamp needed no telling what she needed the bucket for. 'I'll be right back,' he assured her, and went to stand just outside the door for events to develop.

Having heard the door opening and closing, Fflageolet called upstairs, 'Everything alright, Beauchamp?'

'Do you need a hand?' called up Lady Amanda.

'We're fine, thanks,' he called back. 'Just leave us up here until the crisis passes, then I'll let you know what's happening.' There was a commanding tone to his voice that it was as well to obey, but he left the others with all sorts of thoughts going through their minds.

'He can't actually remove someone's appendix, can he?' asked Fflageolet, crediting the butler with considerably more medical knowledge and skill than he possessed.

'Not as far as I know, but you never know with Beauchamp. He has all sorts of unexpected and unusual skills,' replied Lady A, with pride in her voice.

Back up on the landing, there was a considerable amount of grunting coming from behind the closed bedroom door, and Beauchamp stood outside with an impassive face, his mind focused completely on how he was going to get the evidence out of the house without Fflageolet being aware of what he was up to. Presumably, Horseface didn't want what she'd done bandied all over the close.

As he mused on this, a tiny voice from within informed him that 'they' were all out now, and he re-entered the room to find Horseface very red in the face, not just from her exertions on the bucket, but with embarrassment, the contents of the bucket covered with a handful of tissues she had used to clean up her rear end.

'Now what do we do?' she asked anxiously.

'What we do now, is that I call down for my wife, and she sneaks the bucket out of the house – thank God this isn't one of the open plan ones. Is the key still in the lock of the back door?'

'Yes,' she confirmed.

'I'm going to get her to stick it in our outdoors storage cupboard, then come back in and make as if she's coming down the stairs and not been downstairs and outside, or gone anywhere. I'm then going to give her a minute, and flush the lavatory a few times, and go down myself.'

'What about the bucket? Whatever are you going to tell them about it being missing?'

'I'll say I had to have several goes at flushing away what was in it, and it smelled so disgusting, that I put the vomit-soiled receptacle out on the flat conservatory roof for a minute, and that the wind whisked it away, but I'm sure Windy won't mind providing another one, as it was, after all, only a cheap plastic bucket. And I'm going to tell them that you've been sick, rather than tell them what actually happened. Just remember to stick to that story, and we'll be alright. We'll get this sorted together. Then you're going to have to talk to me some more.

'We can't dispose of the drugs, because that will leave your life in danger. What we can do, is clean up the full condoms, and return them to whoever gave them to you, and let whoever it was give them to another mug to take through Customs for him. But it'll have to be in the very near future, because whoever it is, is going to be bound to find out that you haven't actually left the island because of the weather.'

'It was Short John Silver,' she whispered in an almost inaudible voice. 'Can I come and talk to you tomorrow, please?'

'Of course you can. Now, try to get some sleep. You've been through a terrifying experience, and are probably suffering from shock at the cancellation of the ferry and the lack of available direct flights back to England, not to mention the danger from one of the swallowed condoms bursting and killing you.'

'Thank you,' she whispered, shivering with shock, getting back into her rumpled bed, and pulling the thin duvet back over her shoulders, resuming the position in which they had originally found her.

Beauchamp went out on to the landing and called down to those waiting, asking Enid to come up and assuring the other three that they would be able to come up too and see the invalid in about ten minutes' time, and to stay where they were for now.

So worried were the other three that they did as they were told, and Enid dealt with the bucket and its contents, being used to emptying commodes for her elderly mother when she had lived with her. Following her husband's instructions to the letter, she crept back in and up to the landing again, while Beauchamp went into the bathroom and flushed the lavatory three times in succession, also opening the window for a few seconds, and pulling it shut again, just for the sake of veracity. He had no idea how sound would carry in this sort of modern structure, and he didn't want to be caught out in his lies and duplicity.

Closing the door softly behind him, he went down the stairs and told the other four, now that Enid had re-joined them, that Horseface was perfectly alright now she'd got whatever had disagreed with her out of her system, but they'd better leave her, as she was completely exhausted.

'Where's the bucket?' asked Fflageolet, ever vigilant about possessions.

'I'm afraid there was a bit of a mishap with that,' explained Beauchamp, with a perfectly straight face. 'I don't know whether you heard me opening and closing the window in the bathroom, but what was in the bucket did smell foul. I didn't think, and slipped it out on to the flat roof, but the wind caught it as soon as I got it over the sill, and just whipped it away. I last saw it flying over to the jungle, where it'll probably land right in the canopy of the trees and disgust some wildlife with its pong.'

'Never mind. You meant well,' replied Fflageolet, just relieved that her housemate wasn't going to die, 'and it was only a plastic bucket, so it won't cost much to replace.'

Beauchamp sighed with relief, and collected the other three members of his party, leading them back to number eight, where they could have a private discussion without interruption, for who, in their right mind, would disturb a pair of honeymooners?

Chapter Fifteen

Back in the love-nest, the butler told his tale, and Lady Amanda had to be physically restrained from going off to Old Uncle Obediah's Rum Keg Landing Beach Bar immediately. 'We can't go at this time of day while the storm is still high. We have to leave it to when the weather has calmed down and we can confront him without having to shout above the accompanying tympani and lights departments,' he advised, both he and Hugo holding on to an arm each until their temporary captive calmed down.

Beauchamp, ever prepared, made Champagne cocktails, as he knew these soothed the savage breast – or beast, as he preferred to think of his employer – and peace descended once more on the zoned living area of number eight. Finishing his drink rather more quickly than the others, Hugo immediately asked to be pointed at the downstairs cloakroom, was directed to the other side of the dining area, by the patio doors, and toddled off at quite a trot. Champagne did rather run through him.

He was gone quite a while, and Lady Amanda suddenly realised that she had to 'go' too, but not just 'go', but *'go'*, and after a bit of wriggling and squirming, asked if she could use their upstairs facilities. Being answered in the affirmative, she, too, trotted off at a fair lick, to restore her previous level of bodily comfort.

After she had attended to her necessary business, she glanced casually around the bathroom, mentally comparing it to what was available at number fifteen, when her eye alighted on a box, discarded in the wastepaper basket with the name 'Just for Gents' on it. So, she had been right. She had wondered on a few occasions how Beauchamp's hair had remained almost boot-black over the years, and this was confirmation of her deepest suspicions. He *did* dye his hair. This fact gave her enormous satisfaction. So, her butler wasn't quite as perfect as he looked. After all, it could hardly be Enid's for, apart from the title on the box, hers was a mess of grey streaks.

She washed her hands and tottered back downstairs, spearing Beauchamp with a gimlet eye and reminded him that she would soon be in need of her roots being touched up. He had 'blonded' her hair since she had had the first signs of grey taking up residence on her head, but her expression informed him that his secret was no longer withheld from her.

He gave her a withering, don't-give-a-damn look, and informed her that he had discussed it with Enid, and he was going to have a go at jazzing up her hair colour when they got back.

'You'll be opening a part-time hairdressing salon at this rate. You don't want anything doing to yours, do you Hugo?' Lady A asked sarcastically.

'Not on your life!' replied Hugo, his hands rising automatically to cover his thick thatch of white. 'Like that cartoon character, Popeye the Sailor Man, "I yam what I yam", and I don't really want to change anything. I mean, the joint replacement has been great, but I'm happy with how I look. I look like I should for a man of my age.'

'OK, Hugo, don't get your knickers in a twist! I was only joking.'

Shortly afterwards, with an agreement to meet outside number one at ten o'clock the next morning, the two oldies fought their way against the wind across the close to their villa, and turned in for a fairly early night. If Windy called round now, they wouldn't hear her: one, because the noise of the storm was so great, and two, because they were both heavy sleepers, and were quite exhausted after their recent round of activities.

The storm raged for most of the night, wreaking fresh havoc on the island, but by dawn, it had just about blown itself out and, by the time the residents of Parrot Bay woke up, many of them after a disturbed night, not having the capacity of the residents of number fifteen to sleep through anything, the last of the wind was blowing away the cloud cover, and the sky was showing large patches of blue, the sun even making the odd appearance from behind this dreary curtain.

At ten o'clock sharp, the investigating foursome gathered outside number one, where both Horseface and Fflageolet joined them, the former looking rather better than she had the night before. Enid had heroically cleaned the filled condoms from the poo-spattered bucket after their guests had gone the previous night, and given the bucket a good rinse and disinfect.

This, she handed to Fflageolet, after explaining that the five were off on a little stroll, saying that

Beauchamp had found the plastic receptacle up a tree in their back garden early this morning, and they managed to make their escape before the tiny woman could ask them why she wasn't invited, too.

She was somewhat distracted, however, at the thought of actually purchasing the villa the two of them were staying in and, once back there, began to give it a minute visual inspection for any sign of dilapidations that would need putting right before she signed on the dotted line, then she planned to go over to Cocktails to knock around the arrangements for it to be transferred to her name. She was so excited she kept giving little squeaks of anticipation and singing the odd snatch of song.

Horseface, meanwhile, along with the occupants of numbers eight and fifteen, moved down towards the beach to have a confrontation with Short John Silver. Lady A had managed to get them to agree to a short diversion to the beach in slightly the other direction, so that she could show them where Douglas Huddlestone-Black had hidden the dinghy he had obviously used to collect his latest consignment of emeralds. The police would be very interested in that, so they had better just confirm its location. When they got there, however, and Lady Amanda pointed towards where the shrubbery was, under which it had been stuffed, she was dumbfounded to discover that, not only was the dinghy not hiding there anymore, but that there was no longer a large bush for it to be hidden under. The storm must have dislodged the whole plant, and whisked it and the dinghy away to another location.

'That'll be fun, trying to find that, with all this jungle around,' said Enid.

'Not as hard as you think,' replied Lady A. 'it was custard yellow – a very bright colour in case the occupant was swept away to sea in it; easily spotted, and all that.'

'I think we'll leave it to them,' said Beauchamp firmly. 'We've got enough on our plates at the moment,' then clamped his lips shut. Nodding his head towards Horseface, who knew nothing about what Windy and Beep-Beep had been up to.

She, however, raised the subject first. 'I found out this morning that Fflageolet wants to buy the house we're staying in, and Droopy-Drawers wants to purchase number seven, so I suppose things are working out alright for Windy after all.'

All four of her companions treated themselves to a sharp intake of breath, and began to question her about how far things had gone. 'Have they handed over any money yet?' asked Lady Amanda, anxiety sounding in her voice.

'Have they agreed prices?' asked Enid.

'They haven't signed anything yet, have they?' This was Beauchamp, ever practical.

'When are they moving over?' Hugo never could quite keep up with rapidly changing circumstances, and seemed to have completely forgotten how horrified he had been to find out the villas were all part of a property scam.

'Hugo!' Lady A admonished him, and as memory flooded back, he flushed with embarrassment at this lapse of memory.

'What's up?' asked Horseface. Although she was terrified of confronting Short John Silver again, the tone of their questions, and their content had made an impression on her, and she could, even through her fear, hear their disapproval and concern.

'Nothing. Nothing at all. It's just that we'd like a word with the two would-be purchasers.' This was Lady Amanda, reacting rather too negatively.

'Only because there can be surprising drawbacks with actually purchasing in the Caribbean, and they would be better consulting with their solicitors first before they either sign any documents, or commit any money.' Beauchamp butted in, to allay any fears that Lady A's precipitate comments might have fuelled, and Horseface gave him a watery smile.

'Thanks for the heads up. I'll pass it on, and tell them you want to have a word. That's jolly nice of you to give a warning. Ladies on their own can get into all sorts of hot water. I've never spoken to those who've already bought about any problems or obstacles they encountered.'

'Oh, I shouldn't do that,' Beauchamp advised her. 'We'll just have a quiet word, and we'll get everything sorted to everyone's satisfaction,' he said soothingly.

Lady Amanda and Hugo looked at him in amazement, Enid, in admiration. Beauchamp could have made the bubonic plague sound like a minor infection, and the Great Fire of London like a small conflagration in a waste bin. He had such assurance in his voice, and such a golden tongue, that he worded everything just right.

Horseface nodded her head in agreement, and they began moving again towards Old Uncle

Obediah's Rum Keg Landing Beach Bar, in search of the scoundrel who had been part of the drugs ring that had so terrorised Horseface. It wasn't far before they should catch sight of it, but he didn't seem to be there. All they could see looming in the distance was a pile of bamboo and palm fronds, the whole structure flattened by the storm-force winds of the night before.

'Oh, my God! It's been blown to bits,' exclaimed Hugo.

'I wonder if he got out, or whether he's still in there under that lot?' wondered Lady Amanda, quickening her pace slightly, and feeling slightly blood-thirsty. If ever someone was in need of a bit of divine justice, it was Short John. What an evil trade he was involved in, and she rather hoped he had perished.

They made their way as quickly as they could towards the mound of debris, their brains seething with opposing hopes. It was Enid who first spotted the shod feet peeping from under the heavy wooden bar, and she gave a little squeal of shock. 'He's dead. Look. There are his feet, sticking out from under what was the bar top.'

She pointed a finger, and they all followed its direction. 'Come along,' Beauchamp chided them. 'We'd better take a look in case he isn't dead.' It was the only practical solution, but it was a reluctant group that trailed along behind him to discover Short John's fate.

'You lot take hold of the bar and see if you can lift it slightly and I'll grab his ankles and try to pull him out,' the butler said.

'Let's hope he's got strong straps and buckles

on his false ones, then,' added Lady Amanda.

'Let us, indeed, hope that, your ladyship,' agreed Beauchamp, directing the other four to the end of the bar from which the legs protruded. 'Now, after three. One, two, three, heave!' They all heaved as hard as they could, lifting the bar very slightly and Beauchamp pulled as hard as he could on the ankles, which suddenly shot out from under the restricting lump of wood with surprising ease.

'Have they come off?' asked Hugo, with ghoulish interest.

Beauchamp stood looking down at the pair of legs in his hands, a puzzled expression on his face. 'He doesn't seem to have had them on,' he said, perplexed. 'See, the buckles aren't done up,' and he continued to stare at the prosthetic limbs knowing something was wrong, but not being quite sure what it was.

It was Lady Amanda who came up with the answer, causing a whole fireworks display to go off in her head. 'They're not the legs he usually wore,' she almost shouted. 'They're much too long.' Then she lapsed into an excited but speechless silence.

'What is it, Manda? Come on, spit it out,' Hugo urged her, now that he had recovered from his disappointment at not finding the beach bar's proprietor squashed to death under his own bar. What an apt punishment that would have been, after his wicked sideline in drug peddling. Crushed to death by a place that dealt in drugs, but of the alcoholic and, therefore, legal kind.

Lady Amanda suddenly finished her furious

thinking, and began to talk rapidly. 'That's why I always recognised the gait of the tall man I've seen several times. You remember, Hugo, on the beach when Adonis collected his emeralds, at the lagoon when we went there for a swim, oh, loads of times. I knew I knew the walk, but it must have been these legs that put me off the scent.

'His gait was distinctive, because they were false, but he had the silhouette of a much taller man. It was him all along. Was that when he was in touch with you, Horseface?' They might as well get confirmation of this extraordinary claim to identification.

'It was. He told me the legs were hollow, both pairs, so that he could carry drugs with him while he was in the community, but use the taller ones for bigger consignments under the cover of darkness.'

'Golly!' Enid was shocked at this simple act of duplicity.

'He brought some over to the Lizard Lounge that night he helped out, and took it out of his leg in the gents'. That's why all the musicians were having a toke later in the evening. And he knew that if someone saw him in bad lighting, that he was very unlikely to be identified, as the first thing they would notice and report would be his height.'

'What's a toke?' asked Hugo, magnificently naïve.

'Smoking marijuana,' supplied Beauchamp. 'So, where is the wretch now?'

'We could try the Lizard Lounge first, but if he's there, I think we should alert the island's security, rather than try to bring him in ourselves,' said

Enid, ever cautious.

'No, let's see if we can bring him in ourselves. It'll be much more of an adventure, and if we don't succeed, at least we know he can't get off the island, with the sea this churned up.' Lady A was still game for a bit of a tussle.

'It could be dangerous,' Hugo warned her.

'What's he going to do, hit us with one of his other false legs?' Lady Amanda was having none of it. A bit of adventure she had set her heart on, and a bit of adventure she was going to get, and she began to walk in the direction of the Lizard Lounge in a very determined manner. The rest of them followed her, trying to dissuade her, but she was having none of it. She was just in the mood for a confrontation.

'Has anyone met the owner?' asked Beauchamp, anxious to establish whether their accusations would be taken seriously, if the fugitive was there.

'I've met him,' piped up Horseface. 'He's a local who likes to be known as Uncle Tom – God knows why. And he knows that Short John is in the drugs trade, because he keeps him and his staff and some of his customers supplied with weed.'

'Does he now?' commented Lady A, ambiguously, and quickened her pace a little. 'Well, let's hope he doesn't put up too much of a fight for his bit of weed. He'd hardly be treated harshly out here, would he? For a bit of ganja?'

Lady Amanda entered the building first, to find an elderly local, whom she assumed to be the owner, sitting at the bar drinking a beer. 'What can Ah get you, honey?' he asked, with a lazy smile. 'Maybe a little Caribbean cocktail?'

'I'm not here for a drink,' she stated, as the others arrived behind her. 'We're here looking for Short John Silver on a matter of some urgency.'

'And what might dat be, my little bougainvillea flower?' he drawled, trying to exert his considerable charm on her.

'I am nobody's honey or little flower, and we're here to ask him about his drug smuggling activities,' she continued, giving him a steely stare.

'You can't mean de bit of weed that he shares wid his friends and neighbours, can you?'

'No, I mean the hard drugs he tries to get smuggled out of the country for him. I'm talking about his heroin smuggling.'

The old man's face clouded with a disapproving scowl, a figure shot up from behind the bar, and Short John Silver tried to make a run for the back exit. His stumps, however, had become numb during his enforced crouching, and he wasn't too fast, as he couldn't just not feel the legs he had lost, but couldn't feel the legs that he wore either.

Now, on a previous visit, they had noticed that there were some fake parrots perched on hoops, hanging from the low ceiling. Before anyone could move to follow the miscreant, Lady Amanda had jumped as high as she could, caught hold of one of the hoops, and ripped it from its fragile anchorage. She then threw it with the absolute accuracy she had displayed with the quoits when they had been on board ship, and it landed over Short John's head, halting his limping progress. So unexpected was this missile that he immediately stumbled into a table and fell over.

Beauchamp shot over to him like greased lightning, throwing himself on top of the man and calling for something with which to bind his hands. 'I'll need to do his thighs as well, then we can divest him of his lower legs.'

Uncle Tom was sitting muttering about how he didn't approve of hard drugs, but didn't see any harm in a bit of weed now and again, as he hunted out a strong piece of rope from a junk-filled cupboard behind the bar. Lifting his head, he asked, 'Do you want me to go and try to flag down a security car on its rounds?'

'If you don't mind,' Hugo said gratefully. He was unlikely to abscond and leave his business over his receiving a bit of marijuana, and he felt they could trust him.

'If Ah takes mah moped, then if they's not around, Ah can go into de office and get dem,' said Uncle Tom, as he went thoughtfully outside. He had been shocked at Short John Silver's other sideline, and he just didn't approve. Drugs like that ruined people's lives, and even killed them if they weren't careful.

As the captive and his five captors sat in silence, Lady A suddenly voiced her most recent thought. 'If it was this creature I kept seeing in the distance, then it means it was he who saw Adonis collect his little packet of gems. And if that is so, and I also saw someone of his extended build leaving the murder house, then it was probably he who killed our lovely Douglas, because he thought he was muscling in on his share of the drugs trade.

'That's what he would have been searching for

when he pulled out everything in the house. And all he found was that little suede bag, which I came across in a bush outside the front door – where he probably discarded it as worthless. I think we've caught ourselves a murderer as well as a smuggler.'

The security services turned up and were astounded at the story they were told, then dutifully arrested Short John and his legs, both sets. When he had been taken away, Uncle Tom insisted that they have a small glass of beer with him, still expressing shock and horror at what his erstwhile friend had been up to, and turning his mind to whom he could turn, to carry on with his small supply of 'relaxation'.

When the glasses were drained, Lady Amanda suggested that Horseface went back to number one and told the whole story, if she felt inclined to, or just the story of the murder, if she wanted to withhold the information of her being duped into almost being a drugs mule, to Fflageolet. She needed also to warn her not to commit to anything until Beauchamp had had a word with her about purchasing a villa.

'Aren't you coming with me?' she asked, much more relaxed now that she had had her supplier arrested. Hopefully the man who had been trying to blackmail her back home would be frightened off by her telling him that she only had to relate the tale of what was happening on Caribbaya at this very moment, to scare him off for good, and get back her peace of mind.

'We have some matters to discuss when we get

back home,' ad libbed Lady Amanda, half-closing one eye at the others, to alert them that they still had things to deal with here.

The four of them sat on the sand of the beach, which had now dried in the sun and Lady Amanda asked the inevitable question. 'What are we going to do about Windy and Beep-Beep?'

'Why don't we go and wait for the bus to come by, and go into town to the security force's head-quarters, and tell them what the two of them have been up to, for it concerns a lease on part of the island. At least if we could get them arrested, we might be able to get negotiations going with the island's owner about renewing the lease to preserve the homes of those who have already been duped.'

'Beauchamp, you're a genius. Let's get our-selves back to the main road and wait for it to come round. It may be a very roundabout trip, but I don't fancy going back to the close, do you guys? It's almost cost me my sanity since I've known about their duplicity, and yesterday it was particularly hard, biting my tongue.'

'Well said, Manda.' Hugo said, applauding her. 'I really don't think I could face either of them again, or those who have already bought properties, and those who are considering buying. Let's head for that road. It's not too far, but I certainly couldn't have done it before my operations.'

'Hugo, you couldn't even have walked round the close before your operations, not without a Zim-mer frame or two walking sticks,' commented Beauchamp, though in a sympathetic manner.

'Hear hear!' responded Hugo. 'Ain't life grand?'

His face was all smiles as he contemplated the improvements to his life since Lady Amanda had come across him.

Chapter Sixteen

The bus took twenty minutes to come bucketing along the road, and a further forty-five minutes to get to the security firm's office just outside the jewellery quarter, what with its frequent stops to let people off and on, and to wait a few minutes here and there, because a certain passenger was a regular and had probably been held up and Winstone had to wait for them out of a sense of loyalty.

Fortunately their story was believed when Lady Amanda told them that proof of the fraudulent transactions could be found easily in Cocktails itself, and eventually a car was sent out to arrest them. That was good, as they had not been alerted and would not, therefore, have had time – or opportunity with the seas still rough – to flee the island to join their money, wherever they had had it transferred. Maybe, if they coughed up this information, the other girls might even get some compensation. They also said that, as they would have to contact the island's owner, they would apprise him of the situation, and see what he could do about issuing a longer lease, and how much it would cost.

As Windy and Beep-Beep had built the houses out of their original stake and then with the money invested to buy a couple of them, the owner might even let them keep their homes, as there had been no financial cost to him in their erection, and the sale of the remaining villas would be at his discretion. Maybe the compensation received from the fraudulent couple might even cover the purchase of a longer lease.

The officer who dealt with them thought that their case might be considered sympathetically, as the close was a regular source of revenue for the island, and if the rest of the houses were sold, it would only benefit local trade. The Belchester quartet had done as much as they could to help the old school chums, and the rest was out of their hands. Without their uncovering of the scam, two more elderly women would have been cheated out of their capital, and maybe even more in the future, as there were still ten properties unsold.

Having returned to number fifteen after the couple at Cocktails had been taken away for questioning, and with their property undergoing a thorough search, the four of them sat down to a very welcome pot of tea, and a discussion about informing the other inhabitants of the treachery that had been practised upon them.

They had to do no summoning, however, for someone had seen them return and, with the swiftness of any grapevine, word had spread from house to house that Windy and Beep-Beep had been removed in handcuffs and taken away, and that the missing four of their number had returned. They had not even finished their tea when there was a knock at the door and a ring on the bell, and they found that all the others had gathered and come to the house in a deputation.

Horseface, who had been at the heart of the events at Old Uncle Obediah's Rum Keg Landing Beach Bar – RIP – and the follow-up at the Lizard Lounge, had told an edited version of the drug smuggling – minus her involvement in it – and the murder of their darling Adonis, and they now wanted to know what on earth Windy and Beep-Beep had been up to. Surely they weren't drug smugglers as well?

Beauchamp led the explanation of what had happened to the residents of Cocktails, dealing diplomatically but firmly with anyone who got so agitated that they started shouting. 'Let me finish. Let me finish, please,' he called out several times, to the crowd in the sitting room, who became restive and agitated as the story unfolded.

He ploughed through the details, explaining that the owner would be contacted, apprised of the situation, and asked if he would issue a longer lease. If the police finally caught up with the nice little nest egg that the couple had hived off to disappear after, as soon as the sale of their other properties had gone through, there was the possibility of some compensation, to be put toward a new lease. By this time they were much calmer.

The butler finally explained to them that if Fflageolet and Droopy-Drawers still wished to purchase a villa, this would probably have to be conducted through the island's owner, and when he finished, they were in a much more upbeat mood.

It was decided that they would have a celebration, of sorts, that night at number fifteen, to celebrate the sterling work of the detectives amongst them, and then they would keep pretty much to themselves until their date of departure. Things would work out somehow, despite any worrying on their part, and fretting about the situation wouldn't influence the eventual outcome in the slightest.

As they left to go back to their own bases, Horseface hung back to thank them again for their intervention in her terrible dilemma, and to say, with utter horror, that she couldn't believe they had suspected she was indulging in a romantic dalliance with Short John.

'Well, there's no accounting for taste,' Lady Amanda said, stating the obvious.

'Precisely,' replied Horseface, 'I don't even like men.' She gave them an enormous wink and took herself off, back to number one.

'Great Scott!' exclaimed Lady A. 'To think I've been to boarding school with her, and never suspected in the slightest that she might've batted for the other team.'

'What other team?' asked Hugo, whose mind had gone straight to cricket, and who could never pick up a nuance, or follow events quite quickly enough.

'I'll explain it to you later,' she assured him, as she and Enid headed for the kitchen to get something ready for later. Although everyone would bring something with them, it would be as well to have a reasonable spread ready for the first arrivals, so that they didn't look like a bunch of party-poopers.

The shock of finding out how they had been

duped or almost, in the case of some of them, followed by Beauchamp's reassuring words about how the whole mess might be sorted out, produced a hint of euphoria in the old chums, and the party was in full swing when there was a pounding on the door, and Beauchamp answered it, more out of habit than anything else, and revealed the bedraggled and dishevelled figure of Albie Ross. His hair was standing on end and stained black with soot and smuts, as were his hands and clothes, and he looked like a scarecrow out for the night.

'Whatever happened to you?' asked Lady Amanda, joining them to see who this latest visitor was. 'Did someone put you on the top of a bonfire in place of the guy?'

'It's the Parakeet Club,' he said, his voice high and somehow desolate.

'What about it?'

'It only went and got struck by lightning,' he explained, standing firmly on the doormat so that he shouldn't spread soot and dirt around the immaculate hall. Enid handed him a glass with a Blue Lagoon in it, and he drained it in one swallow. 'Ooh, I needed that,' he sighed.

'What's the damage?' asked Lady Amanda, wanting the rest of the story.

'It was struck and caught fire. I've been there most of the night, and all of today too, seeing what I could salvage, but there isn't much left. The whole building's gone, burnt to the ground, and all I've got left are some bottles of booze and the ice-buckets. I even lost all my clothes, because I lived on the premises in a couple of rooms at the back.'

'Take off your shoes and jacket, then come in and go into the downstairs bathroom to get yourself decent. I'm sure our man Beauchamp can sort you out something to wear, while you think about what you're going to do and where you're going to go.'

Beauchamp made tracks to number eight immediately, and Albie disappeared into the bathroom to try to make himself look presentable again. By the time he was clean, dry, and reasonably attired (as Beauchamp's contributions towards his sartorial elegance were a little on the large side), he asked what other news there was.

That kept the old girls entertaining him until nearly midnight, with their tales of the dark deeds of their old head girl and her partner, and of Short John's double life. When they had finished their story, he was not only rather squiffy, but an idea was forming in his head.

'Do you mean to say that the Beach Bar is completely done for?' he asked, hope rising in his voice.

'Just a pile of debris. It wasn't exactly a sound structure, was it?'

'No, but it could easily be rebuilt. It was all bamboo and palm fronds, which I don't exactly have to get from a builder's merchants.'

'True enough,' they all agreed.

'Then if I can get some of the locals to help me clear the site, I can just build another structure like that on *my* site. It's perfect for cocktails before dinner, and I could always scrounge some old tables and chairs,' he decided.

'This is the third establishment you've lost, isn't it?' asked Snotty, sniffing into her handkerchief, as usual.

'It is, sod's law confirms that I've no insurance.'

'Then I think you've just had a very good idea of how to get out of the hole you've suddenly found yourself in,' contributed Hopalong. 'But where are you going to stay until it's ready?'

This was a good point, and one that silenced them all, until Hefferlump's voice suddenly chimed up with, 'You could always stay with me – if you'd like to, that is.'

Albie looked at her, at her rounded figure in its usual T-shirt and shorts, and at her kind face and her snowy white hair. 'Do you know, I think I'd rather like that,' he replied. 'I think I'd like that very much indeed. Thank you very much, dear lady.'

'And please call me Dorothy,' said that lady, looking very pleased with the deal she had just sealed.

'Just make sure there aren't too many sparks flying between you two,' called Wuffles, never very diplomatic. 'We don't want your house going up in flames too.'

Their remaining time on the island of Caribbaya flew by, but allowed Hugo his time lying in the dying rays of the sun, admiring the beauties of the sunset and sipping a sundowner. He finally got his tropical relaxation, without Windy continually organising his time for him, and even went for a couple of dips in the bathwater-warm sea, just for the hell of it, and because he could. He was unlikely to find himself in such a place again, and he had determined to make the most of it.

Beauchamp and Enid retired to number eight to resume their interrupted honeymoon, and Lady Amanda gave Hugo a bit of peace and quiet, as she had got herself involved in the negotiations with the owner about the new lease, and spent any other free time she had badgering the security service, to see if they'd heard anything from the mainland police regarding Windy and Beep-Beep, and the money they had tucked away for their future.

It seemed no time at all before they were boarding the tin cigar to fly them home, all the old St. Hilda's girls who lived there waving from just outside the perimeter fence. 'Well, I'm glad to be going home. It seems an awfully long time since we've seen dear old Belchester Towers,' said Lady Amanda to Hugo, who had a seat beside her in the body of the plane – but not in the window seat, of course.

'Me too, but I did enjoy the last bit, where I really did feel like I was in paradise,' he replied, slightly dishonestly. This was only half the story, and the thing he had enjoyed just as much was the fact that his housemate was so busy with other matters. He was very fond of her, but after the hectic time they'd had it was good just to feel like he was on holiday, with nobody hassling him to go here, go there, do this, or do that.

Chapter Seventeen

Belchester Towers was musty and airless when they arrived home. It had that forlorn appearance that properties adopt when unoccupied for a while. Beauchamp made it his first job, after bringing in the luggage and stowing away the Rolls, to open all the windows and doors to air the place, leaving Enid to provide their employer and her housemate with a pot of tea, before disappearing upstairs to empty the suitcases and other receptacles that had travelled back with them.

She started with Lady A's and Hugo's luggage, sorting the clean from those items that needed cleaning. The former she hung away in the wardrobes, then sorted the more rumpled and grubby items into 'for laundering' or 'dry clean only'.

This task completed, she went into what would be her new abode, to the bed she would share, for the first time, with her new husband, and did the same with their garments. A thrill of excitement ran through her, as she looked at her new sleeping arrangements, the sheets having been changed just before they left for their honeymoon.

With a wave of pure joy, she pulled back the top bedding to air it, feeling slight butterflies in her stomach at the thought of sleeping there, even though they had been together throughout their tropical honeymoon. Tonight was the first night she would sleep beside Beauchamp the butler, instead of with her new husband. It was quite a different prospect. With a little shudder of anticipation, she went downstairs to see what was in the freezer and larder, so that they could eat tonight, thinking wistfully of the small but very important task she had to carry out in the near future.

After opening up the house, Beauchamp changed straight into his butler's uniform, and went off on a property inspection to see if anything had happened that needed attending to while they had been away, also contemplating his first full night with Enid under Lady Amanda's roof with keen enthusiasm.

Enid, having set meat to defrost in a sinkful of water, realised that no one had rung for her to chide her for using made-up powdered milk to go with the tea, and surmised that the other pair were happy to be back, too.

In the drawing room, Hugo was slumped comfortably into an armchair, his cup and saucer on a small table beside him, a smile of contentment on his face. It had been an interesting interlude in the Caribbean, but there was no place like home, and he really felt at home in Belchester Towers. He had known the place for so much of his life, through the friendship between his parents and Manda's, and it had truly become his home since he had moved in. He was happier than he had been for years, he thought, finishing his tea with an audible slurp.

As he put down his cup, he was interrupted in his reverie by the sharp voice of the owner of the property.

'Come on, Hugo; up you get. This won't get the

baby boiled. We never did get that antiques business going. Let's get off and choose a room then you can start rummaging with me. And we haven't got a name for it yet. Got any ideas?'

Hugo sighed, heaved himself into the best approximation of an upright position that he could manage, now that the balmy temperatures were a thing of the past, and stumped off after her, as she trudged out of the room, heading down the hall to the back of the house.

'We'll go through the back rooms first. There are a lot of them not in use at the moment, and we don't want anything too near our living quarters, do we?' Her voice floated over her shoulder to him, and he heaved a great sigh of resignation. She was off again, but at least life was more exciting with his old friend than it had been for many a long year.

Enid left the kitchen and began to visit the rooms in everyday use with a feather duster. Later, she would go round with the vacuum cleaner. She had hated the way her last home had become such a midden, with that manky old cat she had owned, and her mother living with her. She was as house-proud of Belchester Towers now as if it were her own.

Life gradually settled down into a familiar pattern, the only difference discernible, being that Enid was there first thing in the morning as well as last thing at night, as Beauchamp did not have to drive her to and fro now, as he had before they married. She had even bought her sturdy old bicycle with her, so that she could get out and about on her own without disturbing her husband in his duties, which were many and varied.

She was on her way to visit her mother at her sister's house, having left Beechy – as she referred to him – up a stepladder reaching as high as he could with the extending feather duster, into the topmost corners in the high-ceilinged rooms, giving them a bit of a tidy-up. The spiders had really been busy, and if one looked upwards, things were beginning to look a little neglected.

Lady Amanda had dragged Hugo out on an antiques and collectibles hunt, leaving behind her a room at the rear of the house covered in items liberally wrapped in cobwebs and dust-begrimed, which she thought would be the core of her new venture into the commercial world of bygones.

Time ticked by nicely, and it was soon nearly a fortnight since they had returned. They had received information from Caribbaya that the police had tracked down the money that Windy and Beep-Beep had embezzled and they were being prosecuted for fraud. The landlord of the island had agreed to extend the leases and negotiations were on-going with regards to the purchase of the villas. Lady Amanda was delighted with this outcome.

Wuffles had also told them that the emerald smuggling ring had been wound up by Customs and Excise, thanks in part to the information that Lady Amanda and Hugo had given them about the dealer on the island.

It was one afternoon just after luncheon that Beauchamp and Enid disappeared upstairs without a word, and didn't come down for nearly two hours.

'I wonder what they're doing up there?' queried Hugo, musing.

'Probably some unspeakable thing only concerned with married couples,' replied Lady A tartly.

'You don't really think they're arguing, do you?' Hugo's naïvety had depths as yet unplumbed.

'No I don't, you silly...' But she never finished her remark, as the sound of footsteps descending the staircase rather faster than usual was heard. The butler and his wife burst unceremoniously into the drawing room, a wide grin on each of their faces. Beauchamp nearly bursting with pride.

'What is it, you two?' asked Lady Amanda, gazing in disbelief at Enid's hair, which was now a honey-blonde colour and softly waved. She also wore a little lipstick, and looked so much younger, she was almost unrecognisable. 'If it's about Enid's hair, we can already see it. Makes you look so much younger my dear.'

'You look really lovely, Enid,' Hugo complimented her, gazing on this new woman with appreciation.

'No, it's not that, but she does look amazing, doesn't she? I've just been upstairs helping her with the colour and showing how to use the curling wand I bought her, and the result brings out her real beauty, don't you agree?' Without waiting for an answer, he went on, 'She's got something very important to tell you.' At this, his smile grew even wider, and Enid flushed an unbecoming red.

As she hesitated, Lady A chided her. 'Come along, Enid. Spit it out, whatever it is, there's a good girl.'

Enid, squeezing her eyes tight shut, so that she would not witness the reactions of the others, said in a hesitant whisper, 'I'm pregnant. I'm going to have a baby.'

Hugo merely gaped, and Lady Amanda replied rapier quickly. 'But you're much too old. You've always been old. What is this, some sort of immaculate conception?'

'I'm only forty-seven,' she replied, almost as quietly as she had made her previous announcement. 'My hair went grey when I was barely out of my teens: it's a family trait. I guess I just didn't make the best of myself, and settled into old age after my first husband died.'

'Well, you certainly made a good job of it. I would have put you at twenty years too old to be contemplating motherhood.'

'Sorry.' Enid didn't know why she felt the need to apologise, but it just seemed that she should. 'I thought I was going through the change at last, but we've just used a kit up in the bathroom, because I've been feeling a bit queasy in the mornings, and the result was positive.' Enid positively glowed. There would be another baby, but this one, hopefully crying lustily, and not lying still and silent, as her poor stillborn child had lain, so many years ago.

'Good Lord!' said Hugo, with his mouth hanging open with shock and surprise.

'You mean there's going to be a baby in this house?'

'If your ladyship permits there to be,' replied Beauchamp, his fingers crossed behind his back. 'If not, we'll look for somewhere to live, or move back into Enid's old house in Plague Alley.'

'I certainly won't permit that to happen. As long as it doesn't interfere with the smooth running of this house, you are very welcome to stay on here,' replied their employer.

'Good grief!' said Hugo, still struggling to regain his equanimity.

'It'll be quite a novelty to have the laughter of a child livening up these old walls.'

'Good heavens!' said Hugo. 'Although my mother was over forty when she had me,' he added.

'As long as you keep him or her out from under our feet.'

'Of course,' said Beauchamp, breathing a sigh of relief.

'Thank you so much,' said Enid, also crushing the anxiety she had felt at asking permission to stay on, although when she considered the possibility of Lady Amanda throwing out her half-brother, she realised she should not have been worried at all. The idea was unthinkable. She was far too honourable for that.

This momentous occasion was shattered by the harsh ringing of the doorbell, and it was Lady Amanda who went to answer it, Beauchamp being too busy giving Enid a hug of triumph, and Hugo, too stunned to rise from his chair.

She opened the door, and did a double take, whipping round her head to check that Beauchamp was still in the doorway of the drawing room, then back at the young man who stood on the doorstep, smiling politely at her.

'Can I help you, young man?' she asked, taking

in his immaculate state of dress. Maybe it was that that made her think that Beauchamp had just used a time-machine and re-appeared on her doorstep as he looked years ago.

'I hope so,' he replied, his voice refined and pleasant on the ear.

'Does a man named Beauchamp reside here?' he asked, cocking his head to one side to await the answer.

Lady Amanda dithered a bit, before telling him, 'Yes, he does. He is, in fact, my butler. Whom shall I say is calling?' She wasn't used to visitors for Beauchamp coming to the front door, and was momentarily thrown.

'Would you be so kind as to inform him that his son is at the door?'

Turn over for some cocktail recipes:

COCKTAIL RECIPES

Banana Daiquiri

2 measures of white rum
1 measure of crème de banana
1 measure of orange juice
½ a measure of lime juice
¼ of a banana, mashed
1 teaspoonful of whipping cream
1 teaspoonful of castor sugar

Blend all ingredients thoroughly, then add a glass of crushed ice and blend briefly again.
Garnish with fruit and a thick straw.

Blue Lagoon

1 measure of vodka
1 measure of blue curacao
4 measures of lemonade

Mix ingredients, then pour into an ice-filled glass. Garnish with fruit as desired.

Caribbean Sunset

1 measure of crème de banana

1 measure of gin
½ measure of blue curacao
1 measure of whipping cream
¾ of a measure of lemon juice
½ a measure of grenadine

Shake and strain all ingredients except for the grenadine. Strain into an ice-filled glass, adding grenadine last so that it can sink down to the bottom of the drink. Garnish with seasonal fruits as desired.

Grasshopper

1 & 1/3 measures of crème de cacao
1 measure of green crème de menthe
1 & 1/3 measures of whipping cream

Shake and strain. Serve with grated chocolate sprinkles and a short straw.

Martini Cocktail

2 & ½ measures of gin
¼ of a measure of dry vermouth
1 teaspoon of orange bitters – optional

Stir and strain into a frosted glass with a twist of lemon.

Yellow Parrot

½ a measure of absinthe – or Pernod
½ a measure of Yellow Chartreuse
½ a measure of apricot brandy

Shake, strain, and serve.

Happy reading, and happy cocktail hour!

This Large Print Book for the partially sighted, who cannot read normal print, is published under the auspices of

THE ULVERSCROFT FOUNDATION